The Echoes of Yore

LIVIA J. ELLIOT

To Fernando,
who believes in me even when I don't.

Contents

English Language vii
Content Warnings ix

ERYNDOR REGION, CAELANDS
1.1. Renan 3
1.2. Renan 7
1.3. Renan 14
1.4. Renan 25
1.5. Amok 31

ERYNDOR REGION, CAELANDS
2.1. Sian 35
2.2. Sian 41
2.3. Sian 47
2.4. Sian 57
2.5. Amok 63

CORVALEN REGION, CAELANDS
3.1. Cellach 71
3.2. Cellach 79
3.3. Cellach 86
3.4. Cellach 92
3.5. Amok 96

EPILOGUE
Amok 105

Author's Notes 109
About The Author 115

Before you read, please note that my **flavour** of English is mostly Australian. I **apologise** to everyone in advance. Please don't be concerned if you **realise** something is wrong, or think I've committed an **offence**. Who knows, you may even get used to it while **travelling** through the pages.

"Oh, no!" Someone may exclaim, but rest assured, speech quotes remain **double**... at least when someone speaks aloud.

However, alchemists mind-whisper with single quotes and italicised text, 'Speaking directly into someone's mind.'

That said, people think in italics and without quotes: *Just thinking, in privacy. Maybe.*

Also, shall places seem unreachable, you may enquire the **Maps** disclosed after each Chapter cover.

That said, I'm **honoured** that you're interested in my work, and hope you'll enjoy it.

Livia, a writer with Aussie grammar.

This is a speculative psychological horror book following three veterans in a dark fantasy setting. The narrators are highly unreliable and often unstable, which blurs the line between reality and unreality.

You will find depictions of PTSD flashbacks (mostly dissociative) pertaining to veterans, including (but not limited to) explicit limb-loss trauma. As such, there are descriptions of war, bleeding and gore, melee fights, burnt bodies, wolf attacks, animal harm, amputations, healing rituals, and more.

You WILL **NOT** FIND mentions of gender or racial discrimination, and neither of sexual abuse—not on the page, and neither implied. That boundary is deliberate.

Chapter 1

Eryndor Caelands

1470 Bonn Era (BE)

ERYNDOR
GORT DA NAIR
ICRAS
BENVANE
CAERMOR
GLENBRAE
TIRVALE
NANT GWYN
NANT DDU
FAOLWOODS
ABERWYN
SIVARA

Renan

MERCENARY & SWORDSMAN

Noises, dampened. From nowhere to somewhere but all around him. Left, right, gone, back, silence, shouting, gone again.

A scream pierces that nothingness like a spear hissing through the air.

A shadow crashes close to his hands—left open, right fisted around the hilt of his longsword. Both pressing into the ground, framing blood. His blood. It tickles from his mouth; strands of red, of clear saliva, of yellow bile.

Another scream, less muffled, more desperate, and coming, coming, coming— *Parry!*

Renan's longsword meets it high in the air, metal shrieking a death call. He half-kneels, pushes up, twists his grip to force the flat side against the enemy's bloodied edge—a growl building within him. His left palm presses against his own blade and he forces his legs to engage, his arms to push. Up he goes; up, up, up and ahead into salvation, into survival. The other stumbles, exposing his neck; Renan swipes, clean.

Blood spatters onto his face, hot and sticky, churning like the ember-ridden breeze. It burns his sweat, but scrapes his throat when he swallows, bile burning out of him. Heaving, he stands—slouched, exhausted, trembling.

Survive. One vow, with determination tightening his frown. *Survive*, though fire surrounds all, devouring the trees at the forest's edge and sealing the paths between the hills. *No exit*, he knows, spitting a clot. *I'll make one.*

A third scream. It comes at him from behind.

It dies with wide-eyed shock, blood trickling from the now-silent mouth. Renan squeezes the dead man's shoulder, pulls his blade from that chest, and watches the corpse fall back, gurgling. A wall of fire rises ahead, swallowing the forest, creeping over the canopies.

Doesn't matter. His fist tightens around the hilt of his longsword. *I'll make a path.*

The ground jolts and Renan stumbles, pivots to see *them* coming. Mercenaries like him; all bruised, all bloodied, all marked by arm-wraps that once had the colour of their loyalty. All charging because it's an order, because the fire would soon seal their fate, because gold comes only after victory.

He screams, Renan himself. He screams but there is no sound, just the incoming footsteps, the shrill of metal on metal, the crackle of the fire and the char in the air.

It burns like the iron cutting through his maille, through his ribs.

He grips the attacker's wrist, holds it tight—then his own sword-fist raises and plunges, hilt first. It hammers a brow-bone, bloodies itself; jab, jab, jab and a skull shatters, the enemy slipping back, slow and unseeing. Renan kicks at her chest, forces it down with his blade—then pulls it up again, swiping while pivoting, clashing into another then cleaving into a shoulder. That one falls with a lolling head, the next one stumbles and drops on her own, a spear protruding from her back.

They keep coming. Friends, foes, unknown men and women. All marked by the bloodied rags on their arms. Red, red, red— no man's banner, but Death's.

He faces them fully, that raging army coming from the fire and into the fire—and the flames soar, embers cavorting all around them. A grimace twists his mouth, aids him in rolling his shoulders. His heart beats like a war-drum, faster than those madmen racing to clash—but he steps onward, onward, walking at first, then trotting, charging at the mass of—

Water. Droplets only, but so cool, so certain.

Water. Drumming on his cheeks, on his matted hair, on the fist tight around his longsword's hilt. On the field all around, above the battle and past it.

Wrong, so wrong. *Why?*

Rain. It consumes the screams. Sluggish at first, but rushing to replace all sounds, to erase the wind-riding embers, and abolish the tongues of fire. Soft at first, just blurring them all, one flame at a time, one sellsword after. On and on, faster and faster while Renan walks and stumbles, landing knees-down in the mud, weighed down by sudden night-time.

Rain. Strumming onto the leaves, too rhythmic and precise. Digging into the mud, into Renan's cheeks.

It poured from between the pines, through the branches, onto the ground. It rustled through the soaked forest, the wind crisp and cool and sharp and silent.

Silent?

Silent. Why? Renan licked his quivering lips, the coppery, biting tang diluted by water. *No... no, no, no.*

No pain, he noticed. No pain in his ribs, only the one born from realisation. Chilling his shoulders, icy and deadly and shameful and violent because it couldn't be—he'd promised, he'd sworn it.

"No, no, no..." Mumbled; angry. Shaking like his arms. Heavy like his chest. Muffled by the rain, not by the battle that had been. "No! No!!"

Silence, except for the rain erasing his denial and the wardrums pounding on his chest. Killed by his heaving, just before a critter chirped to his right.

Renan glanced in that direction, snarled at it. He couldn't see, for the night and the quiet swallowed all shapes—so he prodded himself instead, sitting on his heels and palming his ribcage. Nothing on the right side, nothing on the left, just the leather wrapping his chest.

Leather. Not maille.

A growl built in his throat, tightened his fists—revealing something trapped on his right. Wrong, so wrong. His jaw tensed, aware of what it was. It flooded him with the disgust and dread that slowed his gaze as he forced it rightwards and down, down, down.

The longsword was in his hand, barely a shimmer of iron blessed by moonlight. The battle was nowhere near—hadn't been either.

Anger. Shame. Indignity.

All mingling, all rising like his blade, like the howl jailed in his throat. All plunging again and again with the violence festering within him.

"Fuck!"

MERCENARY & SWORDSMAN

Twigs cracked under Renan's heavy footsteps, rugged wood pressing into his palms as he stopped by a pine, using it as support. His legs quivered, and his arms wouldn't rest still. He closed his eyes, inhaled the sharp wetness—the petrichor that wouldn't leave even after the rain had long stopped. It cut through his headache, eased that relentless pounding if only for a breath.

Look up, but his body was sluggish, exhausted. More tired than in the aftermath of any real battle. *Look up!* His lids parted at last, gaze focused on the silver blur high above. He was seeking the stars, craving their guidance—but the pines crawled up the sky, branches weaving into a blindfold that left him stranded.

A grunt tensed his mouth into a snarl, his hands into fists. They shook with his anger, with his shame. *At least no one was here*, he thought ruefully, *while I made a fool of myself again*. Yet there was no denying: he was his own witness, and the most unforgiving.

Move, he demanded, snorting when his legs wouldn't obey. *Fool, move!* Pushing himself off the tree challenged his balance, plunging him into another. Something caught his foot, but he trudged forward—one step, one more, one, one, one until he advanced, wrestling the night for directions. It didn't budge, and so his mind wandered while he lumbered, landing in the memories that assailed him.

That battle on the forest of Eryndor's north, survived half a year prior but fought again mere hours ago. The one he'd never wanted nor craved, yet signed for it the moment it was announced.

I should've stayed on The Raven's Howl. He growled, tramping between the trees, seeking the strands of moonlight outlining a path—blurred, like his vision. He remembered the boisterous inn of Tirvale, its warm hearths and endless flow of ale, the laughter and food, and that bed of his own—his reward for his nights on watch. *My life there, I threw it away.* Renan clicked his tongue, crushed a branch under his boots, and plodded onwards. The moonlight shone brighter, as if a clearing awaited ahead—but his legs wouldn't hurry, not even if he demanded it. *Abandoned it. For what?* He couldn't answer that; had never been able either. Then, when the battle had began all questions had floundered away, forgotten. *I had peace, but traded it for a war that doesn't end.* It raged, unyielding—

Hooting interrupted his thoughts, skidding from high above. He looked up to the branches outlined by silver moonlight—but the rustle of wings, departing into the night, gave way to the life of the forest. *The Faolwoods,* though any other detail escaped him.

Renan sucked in a breath, willed himself to walk again—he'd stopped without meaning to, and now his legs were dead beneath him. *Not here. Not again. I must find the caravan to Aberwyn; with luck, it may still be close.* How he'd left it to land in that echo of yore was a mystery to him; it wasn't the first time it'd happened either, just the latest and most inconvenient. He despised himself for it—for inviting that curse, for letting it rage. *I had already retired. Why did I sign up for that lordling's army?* Regret was pointless, yet it festered within him, threatening to dissolve the only dream he'd ever had. The one drifting away every minute that passed without finding the caravan. *Reach Aberwyn's port, sail to Ardmór across the world, then... start anew.*

A new land, a new life. A pocket of this world where perhaps war didn't rage, and he could live his last decade—if he had that much—in peace. *But what is peace?*

The answer wasn't there, didn't matter at that moment.

"Move," Renan hissed through clenched teeth.

Another twig snapped after his first step, another trunk found his shoulder when he traipsed again—but after a while he was trudging. *Move, move, move,* he chanted with every footfall, jaw tense enough to grind his teeth. The trees still had him blindfolded, but moonlight leaked through the gaps ahead; somewhere, beyond the pines, the stars were waiting. *If I can break free long enough to read them and find my way.*

Renan's footsteps scattered between the pines. His body still ached with the fatigue of war, and his arms throbbed whenever he stretched them to part a meddling branch—but his vision no longer blurred, or perhaps the night was too dark to tell. *Keep walking, keep— there!*

His frown trained in the thinning canopies where a patch among the leaves leaked silver light. Another gave way to shimmery hues, and a third twinkled with a single star. By the fourth, Renan stumbled onwards, his legs sore and stiff and too unwilling to hurry—but the hope of finding his way spurred him forwards until he was trotting, slipping on mud, regaining his balance and hurrying, hurrying, leaping over branches, and emerging into a clearing.

A cool breeze brushed his beard, mingled with his heaving. It chilled the sweat on his cheeks, exposed while he frowned at the sky. He'd found the clearing, but the moon's crooked shape was muffled by a shroud of iron clouds—thick, unrelenting, and flashing cobalt with the gnaw of lightning.

No stars. No answers. *No chance of finding the caravan.*

His hand tightened around the hilt of his longsword, its rattle carrying too far. Beyond it rang hollow notes—some calling, others answering. Too measured to be the wind, too alive to be just the forest.

Not good. With effort, Renan lowered to a half-crouch, shoulders so stiff he rolled them before unsheathing his longsword. This time, moving was a necessity, and the need melted the pain away as he stepped into the clearing—where the waning light could reveal an attacker. Five paces in, a low rumble drifted across the dark beyond the trees; two more, and the sky blasted silver and cyan.

Only then Renan saw it.

Darkness absolute, a few paces ahead. It rose from the clearing's centre and absorbed all light into its black stone.

A drulock? Curse my luck! He'd had the misfortune of discovering one before—long ago, on his road to Tirvale—and had promptly deviated as the legends demanded. *No one who stays under one remains alive... or so the Storytellers say.* Yet even knowing the danger he stared at the narrow, doorless tower of iron and stone. He blinked when his vision blurred, shook his head while his heartbeat hammered the night—then stared again. The construction was only two floors tall, yet so black and abyssal it blended into nothingness the moment the lightning eased.

An image lingered in the befalling darkness: cerulean eyes framed by a hooded inky cloak, the wearer standing atop the drulock.

Renan swallowed dryly, stepped back. Murdered a question when a rumbling paced the treeline. Leaves rustled before he caught a warning hiss, and his heart thrummed untamed when breath-backed grunts moved against the wind. *Circling me.* He tightened the grip on his sword, pivoted to stand with his back against the drulock. *Must survive. I've a ship to catch.*

One heartbeat, nighttime.

Darkness all around, the moonlight gone beyond the clouds. Sweat on his hilt, a chill on his cheeks.

Another heartbeat, a flash overhead.

Danger tickles down, cool, deadly. Washing the darkness to pounce on the golden eyes watching him from between the leaves. *Wolves!* Five of them, all around, all about, all growling and lurching as the thunder crashes into the clearing, muffling his scream.

Screams.

They come from nowhere and go somewhere. Left, right, coming, going, gone, coming again. Everywhere and anywhere the battle surges into the plains, roaring war-cries approaching from all around, ushering death in—but Renan sees nothing and just pivots half-right, half-left, left again sword high to parry because the enemies are coming and he can't see them, just hear them.

Death. It chills his neck, slips into him. It awakens something within him.

The screams. They rush from him at last, weaving into the incoming growls.

He parries an axe, hears the rattle obscure a howl and pushes back harder. The woman stumbles back, regains her balance and attacks—but he catches her wrist with his blade, and the axe plummets with a hand tight on its hilt. Red splashes like her screams—loud and louder for three heartbeats, silent after his longsword crosses her neck. Renan heaves, shoulders heavy with— *Look up!* He dodges when a wolf vaults to attack, slashing until mewls and blood rain over and weigh him down—each drop an anchor twisting his chest, pushing and pressing until he howls, his pain scattered in the emptiness of those plains.

It becomes everything; that pressure in his chest. The twisting agony it serves.

Eating his vision away, dampening the sounds, hammering his heartbeat until its gallop is all he hears. Renan stumbles forward—one step, another, another and his longsword cleaves the ground to earn him purchase. Panting, heaving, he claws at his maille, wants to tear it apart to clutch his heart—but he retches instead, heaving, gagging, vision slanting like that pressure choking him to— *Dodge!*

He rolls along the ground, raises his sword. A wolf crowns it, pouring red over him again.

Survive. He throws the animal aside, steps on its ribcage and pulls the blade free. *Survive.*

He can't see clearly. The plains have blurred again, the noon eaten away by the encroaching darkness—rusting the corner of his vision and blurring the rest until only sound remains. The howling, the screams, his own galloping heartbeat.

That something wailing within him.

Survive. Sail to Ardmór. A promise to himself, over and over. *Survive, survive.* A boy charges at him with a spear, impales it in the ground, spins and kicks Renan's jaw—and his teeth chafe, mangling a grunt while his sword-hand slashes up. The scream only leaves him after he plunges and rolls, another wolf now springing towards him. *Aberwyn first, then Ardmór. I must— do... it.*

Teeth sink into his left forearm, rumble a death sentence from between bloodied fangs. Renan bellows, fists his hands, tries to hack with his longsword—but the pressure in his chest sucks the air from him, pulling, wailing, blinding until—

'*Survived s-so many b-battles... only t-to lose... yourself.*' A voice, familiar; younger but somehow old.

It rings over the wolf's grumbling.

It echoes through Renan's thoughts.

Look up, he chides himself, *Look up! Find the speaker!* He does, but everything is dark, darker, blacker—just inky shapes twisting amidst the nothingness past the wolf's golden eyes and the blood in its fangs. Grumbling leaks alongside it, death surging from it while Renan snarls in anger. *Kill it,* he begs himself, sword-arm wrestling that pressure to rise and rise— and his own jaw hinges open too slowly, too sluggishly until a scream tears from it.

His longsword's hilt plummets. Punches the animal's muzzle, cracking its upper jaw and cracking it again and again and again until everything is carmine and the blade is forgotten because his hands find the wolf's neck and he's choking, chok- ing, tighter, screaming, soundless, quiet.

'*You persist... and t-that is-s...*' That voice again; distorted. Wrenching Renan's chest, tearing it apart with every word. '*... your— only accomp-plishment.*'

Renan shouts, stumbles again, free hand seeking his chest, clutching the maille to free his heart. His eyes dart in the noon- darkness, scampering through the blurred shapes. He searches, he pants, he finds it at last.

The speaker.

Just a shadow of a man, amethyst strands coiling from it like smoke. It's shapeless, just a humanoid, limbless mound with silver eyes like his own—but it waits there, taunting, chiding, the smoke soaring until it's gone and a hundred mercenaries flood the plains.

Shrieking, howling. Behind, ahead, circling, gone, here again —between his heaving and the heartbeat that gallops unyielding. *I'll survive. Reach Ardmór.* Renan spits blood, clutches his chest while he picks up his longsword.

Only then the battle begins.

Renan

MERCENARY & SWORDSMAN

The sun surged like a vibrant copper disc; bleeding into a sky that welcomed it by pouring liquid gold into its wounds. The griadergh,[1] the Blood of the Sun, reflected amaranth into the clouds—now moving away from the Faolwoods to reveal the sky beyond, tinged bronze like a shield that'd never break.

Renan grimaced at it, slumping down on a stone at the edge of a current. His legs throbbed as he stretched them, still gauging the sun. It was dawning from downstream, and that only meant one thing. *This river is not Sivara.* That one flowed south, while the one near decanted east towards the griadergh. *It could be the Nant Ddu, the southern branch of the Nant...* He assessed its narrowness, glanced at the clear water. *No; more likely a nameless stream.* A grunt built at the back of his throat, pulsing in his aching jaw while he rubbed his face. *I've strayed too far north.*

Removing the longsword's sheath from his belt, he knelt down to cup water and splash his face. It hit hard and cool,

---

1. Author's Note: *Griadergh* was derived from *grian* (old Scottish Gaelic for 'sun'), and *derg* (Irish for 'red'). It roughly translates to Blood of the Sun—the name of dawn. While I'm aware that blending words belonging to different languages is not the most linguistically correct approach, this is a dark fantasy setting—and when creating the words of this world I chose to mix in this way whenever I wanted to imply some mix of cultures.

itching on his parched lips and washing his exhaustion. He cupped some more, slapped himself again with it, then drank the remnants.

Miserable idiot! Renan spread his palms open, fisted them until veins flared in his sun-kissed skin. *It was too soon for another echo. Too soon.* He wanted to crush the past, shatter it until it wouldn't haunt him anymore—but he couldn't catch it, couldn't erase it either, just endure its recurrences until the Spirits would take him. *It's my fault. If I hadn't—*

Silver eyes fixed on him from under the stream. A shadow spread beneath them.

Renan blinked, lowering his fists. Those eyes didn't shift, and his hands… they hadn't reflected at all.

His breath hitched, halving the silence. He blinked again, dropped low to brush his fingertips on the hilt of his longsword —then peered at the stream.

Silver eyes on black, and a stare that chilled him to the bone.

His lips pressed into a line, fingers curling around the hilt. His eyelid twitched, his cheek, half his lip. All stressed by his heartbeat, limping here and there, eating the corners of his vision while those eyes—those silver eyes—stayed on him. Haunting. Hounding.

Critters rustled on the bushes. Something hooted above the treetops.

Renan did not move, did not breathe and just stared, drawn to the silver on black.

The griadergh cast its bloody shimmer over the water's surface—and realisation slapped him back into reality.

He grimaced, and so did his reflection—lost for a moment as he dropped the longsword and peered again. A mirror of his own silver eyes met him, blinking and squinting when he did. His head obscured the water, dimming the shape of his bushy pale brows, barely darker than his hair. Mud, grass, and wolf's blood darkened some strands, sticking them to his forehead and temples.

Pathetic! Renan splashed the water, smearing his reflection. *What was I thinking!? I thought it was that shadow from last night!* He watched the ripples quell, the surface slowly mirroring the coppery sky. Only then did he peer again, squinting left and right to study his profile until what remained was just the chills on his nape. *I hadn't seen anything like it until last night...* He recalled it only vaguely, or perhaps not at all. It had seemed humanoid, but could've been a hooded mercenary, an assassin, or just his imagination. *My mind is... fraying faster than—*

A growl, loud. His, and reluctant.

Then he hauled water into his hair. Once, twice as he worked through the clotted blood, cleaning himself. *The caravan must be long gone by now. I'll have to walk to Aberwyn.* Grime dripped through his temples and cheeks, forcing him to rinse his beard and moustache. He worked them methodically, considering his journey south—walking aimlessly was not an option; he couldn't afford to stumble into the drulock again. *I can use the griadergh and nefrudh[2] as guides... and at night, I may watch the stars.* He looked up at that moment, rolling his sore shoulders and imagining where Draighal, the noble dragon, or Artanem, the sky-bear, should be.

The breeze dried him as he stared, each droplet tickling down his face like a chilling reminder of what he sought to avoid.

Yet his worries refused to be forgotten.

How long did I fight last night? And how much of that was real? Those worries weighed him until he dared to study his left forearm. The vambrace was cleaved with bitemarks—shaped like half-moons and stained with dried blood. *The wolves were real... or at least this one was.* A snarl twisted his mouth; his skin aflame while he unfastened the straps and peeled the leather away. Rolling his sleeve lynched his skin, yet it only revealed shallow dragmarks—shaped in another half-circle, bloodied and bruised purple but otherwise superficial. *Lucky. Too lucky.*

Renan cupped more water and splashed it over the bite, fingers twitching and fisting as if to contain the fire bursting from it. He set his jaw and scrubbed despite the pain, the itch spreading under his skin the longer he washed. His teeth chafed

---

2. Author's Note: *Nefrudh* was derived from *nef* (Old Welsh for heaven) and *rudh* (Old Welsh for 'red'). It roughly means Red Heavens—the name of dusk.

when clean bandages grazed the wound, but he worked through the itch, covering the bitemark. Only then did he rinse the vambrace, thumb working the leather until it was clean enough —then fitted it over the wrappings. The straps gnawed down and he hissed, tightening and easing until the sting faded to a throb.

He studied it for a moment, then fidgeted with the same belt-scrip where he kept some bandages—*three more; enough to change my wrappings on the road*—and produced a small pouch of jerky. He opened it before his stomach grunted, picked one and savoured it. *Not enough; only a few left*—so he devoured them, aware he'd need to hunt soon. As he finished the meagre food, his fingers flattened the pouch and slipped it back into the scrip.

Shouldn't dally. Aberwyn awaits me, though he leaned in to drink more water and refill his waterskin. Travelling by day would be safer, he knew it—yet he wouldn't leave that stream, wouldn't walk, wouldn't even try.

"Move!" One order, shouted.

Birds fled from the canopies, breaking the silence.

Spirits... steady me. Renan finally turned, tying the waterskin to his belt. Five steps—and he halted again.

The shadow stood paces ahead, just as he'd seen it the night before. A humanoid mound of darkness, strands of amethyst smoke streaming from its body. Those didn't react to the breeze, didn't bend nor bulge—just oozed, so slowly, so scentless.

Renan dared to reach for his longsword. *Please—*

A wrenching force held onto his heart, tearing. He gagged, stumbled forth, forgot the blade and clutched his chest—but the pressure was mounting, spreading, eating his body until he gasped for useless air, gasping and gasping without breathing. He groaned, punched his chest to dislodge the pain, then punched it again. It stuttered, erratic but traipsing, trotting, faster, rushing, spreading to pound on his temples, on his forehead, on his vision until the corners darkened and writhed, coiling towards that shadow-mound.

Silver eyes opened on black. Stared at him fully, framed by those amethyst coils.

Silence reigned in the forest, hammered down by the war-drum on Renan's chest. *Not now... not again...* It augured an army, drove that wrenching force deeper into his chest until he was certain that Death was upon him and wouldn't miss this time—it'd bring him to the past to kill.

Silver eyes writhed.

Ahead of him, the shadow twitched. It paused, craned the head, swivelled again and shaped a mouth to howl. No sounds, no words. Just an open gap. Just the jerking and trembling and violet strands pulling and twisting the stump that finally grew into an arm. Flailing, stiffening, flailing again and shaping a hand that clutched the other shoulder stump.

Renan fell to a knee, pressed both palms to the ground. *Not... like this.* Blood leaked from his nose, slipped through his moustache and into his lips. Sharp, metallic. Dropping constantly, carmine over the dark grass; spiralling, spiralling fast, faster still.

Run, he demanded of himself. Fought to obey his own command. *Run to Aberwyn.*

His body did not comply, did not move. It lingered, weighed down, unresponsive though his nose bled and his heart sprinted like he wished to do. *Run.* He craved it: to escape, to flee to Aberwyn and its port, sail to Ardmór and a decade of peace. *Run.* He begged, heaving, each intake sharp as a dagger under that mounting pressure. *Run. Run!* Again. Against the burden crushing his chest, against the strain twisting his mind and wrenching him apart.

"Run!" One howl. Will made true.

One step to raise, one stumble to lurch, two more for balance, and a handful faster until Renan broke into a trot. Past the one-armed shadow and into the trees, faster and faster until the bushes hid him and the treetops thickened again.

The shadow didn't chase him.

Renan lumbered on, exhaustion bending his posture. His pace dragged, his knees locked and unlocked until one foot clipped the ground and he staggered, arms windmilling before he caught himself against a trunk. His breathing came in rags, the air useless even though he dragged it in mouthfuls. He'd let fear carry him farther than what his body should've allowed, but whatever that shadow was... he had to leave it behind. *It... it grew an—*

That mouth-gap. It had opened and screamed, but only silence had come.

"What—?" Renan's heaving choked his question. "—was it? What!?"

Don't think of it. Forget it. He shut his eyes, willed that image to vanish, then looked up. His vision tunnelled, black patches blasting across until he blinked and finally caught the sky. *Forget the rest. Focus. What does the sky say?* Partly obscured by the pines' canopies, it shimmered buttermilk and bronze, with no traces of clouds. *That's it. Just an hour or two after dawn.* But the black took over the light again. Renan grimaced, looking down—he'd stopped without wanting to, and his exhaustion sent the forest into a spin.

Heavy, heavier with each twist. He folded over, hands trembling when he braced them on his knees. Every breath scraped his throat, every waft of breeze chilled his nape, hollowing his gut until he retched, spitting blood and bile. He swiped his nose with the back of his hand, massaged his chest though the leathers stifled his motions—the pressure wouldn't ease, fraying the bonds inside him. *Can't lose myself now. Not like this.*

The forest's silence absorbed him, time drifting away.

Must walk; can't stop. Renan pursed his mouth, forced his breathing to ease while wishing for the waterskin. One glance, licking his lips, craving the water—but he left it untouched on his hip. *Not now; don't know when I'll find another stream.* A painful decision, but he endured it while he pushed himself off the trunk, staggering until his sore legs settled into a rhythm— not fast, not quick; just constant.

Through the pines, between the bushes, and far away from any road. *Straight south towards Aberwyn; two weeks, and I'll be there.*

Saliva dangled from his mouth; Renan sucked it, licking his lips. The splotches of black covering his vision had long melted into blazing, iridescent circles—burning behind his eyes and blurring whatever he looked at. They worsened in the shadows, and so he walked with his gaze trained in the shafts of honey light pouring from between the branches.

Spirits, have mercy. His gait had reached a rhythm during the last hours, though nothing more than stumbles interspersed with a few measured steps. It took him deeper into the Faol-woods and hopefully south, but always through the greener, more illuminated patches. *That shadow may—*

Movement on the bushes. Right, and mere paces away.

Renan halted, one hand reaching for his longsword's hilt, the other still pressing his strangled chest. The breeze danced through the pines, lifting a fresh, tangy scent. It tickled on his nape, under his beard; the sweat had dried, but the chills returned, itching until he shivered and rolled his shoulders.

Just a hare; nothing else, he told himself, though his legs refused to move and his gaze surveyed the greenery. Hunger snarled in his gut, raw and hollow and cutting through the latent weariness that kept him awake. *I should kill it; eat something.* His stomach twisted again, refusing to be ignored. Renan lowered his hand, pressing it uselessly against the ache. *Haven't eaten in... what? Two days? I can't fast until Aberwyn; it's too far.* He looked back, didn't catch a shadow; looked ahead, took in the quiet. Slowly, he edged closer to—

'Coward.' A man's voice; it reached him from no source.

Close, too close.

Renan groaned, unsheathed his longsword and pivoted. Quick, left, right, half-right, half-left, stumbling back, left again, snarling, backtracking. His back hit a trunk, drew a grunt. *Where?* He looked ahead, longsword held high—frowning at his left, at his right, all around. The iridescent circles still churned behind his eyes, ravaging his vision. *Spirits, where!?*

It was there, the shadow he'd seen hours ago. He knew it. Felt it on the cold sweat chilling his neck, on the breathing that came in sips. Rapid, panting, sip, sip, sip in tandem with his heart and that pressure that never eased, just wrenched and tore until he punched his chest thrice in a row. One. Two. Three.

Silence.

A breeze sneaked through the Faolwoods, fresh and sweet. Leaves rustled as it picked up, the shafts of light swaying until it eased and silence reigned again.

Nothing lurked. No animals, no hares, no birds. Just the leaves.

Renan did not move; did not believe the forest.

He waited—glancing into the corners, releasing his water-skin and downing three gulps before tucking it again on his belt. His tongue darted through his lips, ravenous as it caught a few droplets... and his gut clenched, begging for food. He ignored it, pushing himself off the trunk and marching again. *I won't fray. Not now, not ever.* Faster than before, with a lousier rhythm and more stumbles. *I'll reach Ardmór and settle there. I'll find peace.* His heart insisted on its reckless galloping, each pulse cinching his chest tighter and tighter—but Renan lumbered on, gait contorted by swerving through brushes and branches to—

'Weakling.' The voice again. Sourceless.

Renan sucked in a breath, spun twice and saw nothing but the shafts of light. The Faolwoods mocked him with its peace and silence, its beauty churning while his vision tunnelled again. Desperate, he clutched his chest, massaged it because it felt crowded—with no room left for him in his own body.

"Sod off..." he snarled at the forest's emptiness, turning again.

This... must be just another echo... he chewed his lips, picking up his pace. *I won't fray. I won't.* He pushed through the pain and dragged himself forward, moving a branch and swerving around a bush. *I'll die in Ardmór, after a decade of peace.* He looked over his shoulder, imagining the lands he'd acquire—but the Faolwoods held him back. *Walk,* he ordered himself. *Walk to—*

A hiss slithered through him, chilling his neck, tearing his breath apart. It coiled like a serpent around his heart.

Renan gasped, clutching his chest with both hands—his heart pounding as if it now answered two masters.

'So... *weak.*' The shadow's voice. There, not-there, everywhere. '*What a w-retched... t-thing you— are...*'

It wrenched within him, that pressure on his chest. It tore and tore and Renan groaned, scraping his chest, scraping some more. Right and left, right, left, faster, quicker, shorter like his breathing—pulling air that gave him nothing. He arched forth to gag, then back to scream and instead huffed, heaving, huffing with a hand holding his throat to dislodge whatever choked him.

Light blinded him.

Renan fell forward. Howled in silence. Warmth dripped from his mouth—yellow and acidic, red and metallic. Yellow, red, yellow, red, stuttering and stumbling like his pacing.

"Mo... ve..." Panting yellow and red. "Farther... away..."

Away from that voice, from that echo that augured another army. Away from the pain and into salvation, into survival.

Darkness moved above.

One grunt—he looked up, sucked in a breath.

Darkness moved closer.

Renan spun, spun again, traipsed on a branch, fell with a cry. He rolled, half-crouched with knees bent, fingers splayed on the forest floor, gaze cutting from pine to pine, from bush to leaf to the shafts of light. They fluttered, like the world—rippling while those iridescent circles churned his vision away.

Fire built within him; acrid, burning. Pulsing on his gut, wrenching his chest apart and pulling something through his throat until he retched. Bile leaked from the corner of his mouth—just one strand, dense and unbreakable even as he panted. He swiped it with his hand, swiped his beard as well and rose until his hands pressed into his knees, all of him trembling.

He looked up—to the forest, so quiet, and the shafts of honey light.

Nothing; *just* the forest. No hares, no birds, no vermin—not even flies, drawn to his sour sweat and musk. He believed the forest even less.

I'm fraying; I won't last, Renan decided, panting and looking around. Frowning at the bushes, snarling at the leaves flirting with the breeze. *Too many echoes, too soon. Nothing's real.* He saw nothing but the pines, just dark green leaves and shafts of honey light. *Not even the forest.*

Yet he couldn't move.

Something had lodged in his chest, weightless but suffocating. A pressure that wrenched and twisted and wrung him over and over to peel and peel and peel. His mouth quivered, shaped a snarl, a grimace, a howl—all silent, all so slowly blending from one to another that he tracked that sole drop of sweat trailing down his temple while the pressure thickened, deepened, expanding to be everything.

The forest darkened; his vision ate it. From the corners inward, like fire charring paper. Only one spot remained, narrow, narrowing.

There. Walk, he thought, chewing on his lips until he drew blood and swallowed it. Bitter, metallic; compelling enough his right foot pressed forward. *Keep south.* He sloshed the blood in his mouth, pressed his chest with a hand, the ground with his other foot. *South to Aberwyn.*

Chew, blood, step.

Again.

Again.

He stopped, grimacing.

The shadow awaited him, streaming the amethyst smoke. Two-armed, half-turned, and watching its palms.

"No…" The mutter tumbled from Renan's lips—just before he chewed them again. "No, no, no…"

He had seen that gesture before; he sees it again.

That woman, standing alone at the edge where the town ends and the oak forest begins. Clad in char and cinders, her black hair burnt to the scalp. Staring unblinking at her hands, tilting her head and hinging her jaw—screamless. No echoes, no sounds; not even as her knees scrape the ground and she howls again, back so curled she's a ball of rags and grime. Silent; so, so silent.

Only then Renan sees the others.

Corpses, all. Hanging from the oaks; two per branch, so many they are. All swinging in a lazy cadence, half-circles, some in tandem, others colliding. Some are smaller—too small, but not small enough for war—others so broken they are mere carmine slabs.

"Benvane…" The town's name. He remembers it now, curses himself for his lateness.

If he'd come, if he'd hurried, if he hadn't partied in that inn—perhaps, perhaps…

'Useless…' That voice; it comes from the charred woman but echoes all around. *'You want t-to… live but… can't live, j-just… remember.'*

Look up, and he sees the woman near the oaks, mourning.

Pain swells in his chest—and he stumbles again, arms flailing until he drifts and gains some purchase, his hand pressed against a hanging corpse. Acid churns within him, his chest twists and coils and he pants, huffs and heaves but breathes nothing. Over and over though he scrapes and scratches and the maille shrieks and carries hollow notes. He punches his chest harder and harder, stopping to gasp, to shake his head and punch again—but light blasts iridescent through his vision and his knees sink to the ground.

Blood. Saliva. Bile.

It pools between his hands.

Look up. One order, so difficult to obey. *Look up, look up.*

Renan closed his eyes; opened them again. Glanced left, right, up.

It wasn't a woman dressed in char, but a humanoid shadow with a violet shimmer—outlining two arms, two legs, and a longsword sheathed at its hip.

It was the shadow, and it was real.

Amidst the darkness as he drifted away.

Renan

MERCENARY & SWORDSMAN

Aberwyn... isn't far. I must... reach it.

Light, pouring down. Fraying gold and brilliant and blinding.

Sail to... Ardmór.

Nothing around, just his pain. Just the pressure swelling his chest and leaving no space for air. He grunted, saw nothing but splotches of black and those shimmering, iridescent shapes.

Darkness overwhelmed him.

Aberwyn. Sail. Ardmór.

Light, bleeding from the sky. Gushing from between pitch-black leaves.

Peace after.

Soreness churned in his gut, blazed through his arms. He gasped, but the air wouldn't fit inside his chest. Shadowy feet stepped from him. On him.

Something crouched to watch him drift into an abyss.

Eat, rest. Reach Aberwyn.

The grass was moist under his palm, yielding as he pushed. He carved a handprint, smeared it with his torso when he dragged onwards—through one, then another.

I'm not far; just... one, two weeks on foot.

Three more handprints and he pushed with both hands, raising himself to see his face reflected on the springlet nearby. It was a shallow pool over a greyish rockbed dotted with moss, its water crystalline and peaceful—offering a near-perfect reflection.

I'm not... fraying. I can hold.

Renan scowled. Only half of his face scowled back.

Trust nothing.

Dragging his knees under him, he leaned to wash his hands. Rivulets of murk and grime oozed downstream, smearing his image. He watched it, impatient as the water settled and mirrored him again—then pursed his lips, frowned with effort. The right side of his face reacted, but the other lagged, lazy and uncooperative.

Not fraying. This... will heal. His grunt was half-hearted, sore like the rest of his body—yet he edged closer and downward to drink from the springlet. He washed his face, splashed water in his wolf-bitten arm just in case—then dragged himself up to stand against a trunk.

That northern frontier town drifted back to his mind. *Benvane... That's the name.* It was carved into his memory, even after a decade. *The war that doesn't end. The echoes of yore.* He clicked his tongue, rubbed his face with water-cooled hands— then watched his palms. *That woman...* To him, she'd never been whole, never truly human; just a mound of char and cinders, mourning near the oaks. Just darkness—

The shadow.

First a humanoid mound, then a slab with limbs... and lastly a swordsman. Just a featureless silhouette, oozing that amethyst smoke to eclipse the mid-morning honey-light—yet something of its bearing lingered like an afterimage. Alive, maybe, but known. *Its stance... was familiar. Too familiar.* His eyelid twitched, then his upper lip. *Familiar because—*

"Nonsense," Renan muttered, pushing himself away from the pine.

His legs quivered under him, tingles tickling through his knees—but he stretched them, holding himself against a branch and shaking his feet. One, the other, then he crouched near the springlet and refilled his waterskin. It gurgled, bubbles bursting while he looked at the Faolwoods—the afternoon was young, more than enough to find game. *Must eat; gather something for the journey.* Corking the waterskin, he strapped it to his belt and stepped—slowly, carefully—downstream towards a narrower section.

An exhalation; that was all it took.

Renan staggered, all strength removed from his body.

His foot clipped the path, a grunt knotting in his throat. He folded, catching himself bent over—his chest so swollen it barely fitted him, his heart so confused it skipped, trotting, leaping, no semblance of a rhythm left. His breathing ragged, rusting and clawing for air, but suffocating all the while. All sounds were muted except his war-drum of a heart; all colours gone except the red, the black, the silver swirling like blood on water.

The breeze scraped his neck, gave him nothing but a name. His name.

His heart vaulted—and something caught it mid-beat.

Whatever that was it cleaved, wrenching half of him forward, the rest pushed back into the howl he never roared. His lungs fought for air, his hands for purchase and found his chest—gripping nothing, scraping the leather. That thing yanked, choking Renan with grief and loss and an emptiness that filled him when before he'd had no room for himself.

All sounds vanished; even his own.

No leaves rustling. No water running. No heartbeat, no panting, no leather scraping, just deafening silence.

Just silence, and the colours bleeding red-black-silver through his eyes like the hues of wrath, shame, and defiance behind his snarl.

Just silence, and the shadow standing ahead, amethyst smoke coiling from it like the fight twisting within Renan.

'You can't... t-trust your own reality.' It spoke in the silence. *'Never... c-could.'*

Renan's leathers rustled. Tsk-tsk-tsked when he scraped with just three fingers. Marking a tempo, a countdown.

"Leave..." He growled, his anger barely moving past his parched lips.

The shadow chuckled, the mockery towering over him though the shape hadn't moved—awaiting four paces across the springlet, longsword on hand. Violet shimmered at its edges; contempt oozed from its presence.

A witness, that it was, and the most unforgiving.

'Leave? I'll n-never... leave...' Its eyes, they blinked once when they'd never shifted before. *'I can't l-leave... your d-disgrace.'*

Truth. Untruth.

Both.

Neither.

Leather scratching. Renan couldn't decide; he knew the answer but refused and scratched instead. Left, right, left, right. His wrath itched, his pain swelled, that wrenching returning while he scratched, fast, faster, wrenching, clutching, clawing, clawing, fury, defiance, claw, claw, claw, scream, silence. *Spirits...* Hands on his neck, choking, scribbling. *...steady me.* Hands on his heart, breaking, tearing, pulling him apart, holding him whole. *I'll... hold.* The shadow ahead, standing in a way he no longer did.

"Liar." Shame, regret, swirling like bile and blood on clear water, muddying his voice, muddying his mind, so unforgiving. "You'll leave—"

A woman shrilled. Pitched high, terror leaking into a wail.

Silence. Then, the echo.

Renan gaped, not clawing, not scratching, just watching and reaching for his longsword, head tilting as if that shrill would again fall into his ears. Laughter came instead; men, women, young all of them, voices smooth over the rhythmic clash of blades; someone's voice, then metal on metal. Over and again, over and again but gone. Laughter, but it wrecked into the frantic roaring hammered by a charge towards death and the enemies that'd meet it. Colours rose from behind the screams—

banners, some green, others blue or purple or red with lions and wings and shapes.

Wrath, amidst it all. Wrath in his swollen chest. Wrath, wrath, wrath because that shadow wouldn't leave him alone and instead pulled and pulled, fraying what remained of him, what he'd promised to hold on to.

It pulled again, from within him.

Shearing, tearing, streaming him away until Renan staggered, drew his longsword, cleaved it into the ground—folding over it because its hilt was an anchor, and he was bowing to mint an oath. *Kill it. Survive. Travel. Peace.*

His chest was hollow; his mind, hollower.

But that oath remained. The journey awaited.

"I'll… reach Aberwyn…" Words dripping with blood. Streaming from his nose, pouring into his moustache and lips. "You can't… fray me. I'll leave… Caelands. Reach… Ardmór."

He looked up, blinked until the red-black-silver swooshed aside and among the pines and the banners he found the shadow-swordsman—waiting paces after the springlet, longsword on hand but utterly still. Only the amethyst swayed, but never in tandem with the wind.

'Can't… stop. You.' The shadow blurred, edges churning violet. Smoke surged again. 'You… *at war w-with— against… you.*'

Wrath, and the oath.

Pouring into Renan's howl. Refracting in the pines, fracturing into thinned remnants amidst the peace and quiet only he had perturbed. It tore into broken wails—anger, shame, regret, one shard after the other but coming and going and coming and going yet always leashed, always there.

Kill it. Survive. Travel. Peace. He'd promised, he'd sworn it.

Iron slashed the wind, hauled up, caught the skylight and bounced it buttermilk. It rested on Renan's shoulder, rattled with his panting.

One breath. *I'll kill it.*

Another breath. *Stop the fraying.*

Renan lunged, aiming his longsword, locking his gaze. Silver on silver, bootfalls over water, water on his calves. Murk on his soles, terror on his mind. Half of him ahead, half of him reaching for it. Death coming and waiting.

Heavy, heavier, each footstep, each moment. Crushing his chest, wrenching him still. Grunting, with effort, with despair, with an oath.

Honey sunlight, bathing his blade, sinking into—

Amok

SOUL TRANSMUTER ALCHEMIST. THE UNTAMED ONE

Golden light coruscated between the pines—refracting on the murky, inky leaves, on the greyish water of the springlet, on the iron of that sword resting against the grass. It was a tool of destruction, a survivor of menial wars, a killer of pointless lives —and it had defaced something its owner couldn't fathom.

Amok recognised what had led it. The invariable need to destroy the unknown, a trait innate to humankind. They dreamed of evolution and understanding, yet sought to obliterate the Uncharted because their ignorance bred fear, fear compelled violence, and violence created the illusion of power. No matter the world, no matter the age, no matter the laws and creeds, humans existed in a perpetual cycle of self-destruction and self-preservation.

Yet on that eve of a blood-stained dusk, Amok suspended their displeasure for the sake of doing what humans could never do: learning.

Intrigued, they hovered down until their feet grazed the dark grass, their footfalls silenced by will alone. Their cloak of liquid ink swayed as they rounded the body splayed face down on the ground, a myriad of cerulean glyphs swarming around them to record their observations.

The subject had collapsed lifeless after piercing the Shadow, his right hand forever gripping his longsword's hilt. His face—

and Amok crouched near to close the distance—was locked in a silent scream, pale grey eyes open and unseeing.

It was a look of utter misery and despair, never marred by the shock of his unplanned suicide. After all, the subject had died by killing part of himself—the embodiment of shame and self-directed anger that Amok had attempted to *incarnate* out of him. The only pain captured in that face was due to enduring the alchemist's attempt at wrenching those emotions and associated thoughts—all of them alive elements—out of him.

Yet the human's self-murderous intention had been unexpected—an impulse the alchemist had allowed as part of their Naturalist process, and solely due to what it may reveal.

The result had been expected. Whereas the Untamed One had selected the subject because of his advanced dissociation, it'd muddied the experiment and led to premature collapse. That human had been, without a doubt, too fragmented for this venture—his mind already fraying past the point where past and present collided without distinction into a single experience.

A unique suicide, the first of its kind in the history of Soul Alchemy, and an intrinsic part of the trial and error that would eventually lead Amok to perfecting the *incarnate*—that nascent soul-skill they'd theorised more than a millennium ago and had researched since then.

A minor success, since for the first time, the alchemist's attempt had resulted in a somewhat realised Shadow—one that had lasted enough to communicate, even if only to the subject's mind. Success indeed, albeit partial due to two impediments to be corrected during the selection of the following subjects: his lack of bodily tolerance, and his lack of curiosity.

Standing again, the alchemist rolled two fingers and their glyphs blazed aquamarine and cerulean, documenting their findings. Some shimmered into dull red, rejecting new hypotheses, while others moved in clusters to connect ideas. It'd been an informative experiment, indeed—but there was still much to test.

After all, experimentation demanded that only one small change be made at a time.

Eryndor Caelands

1471 Bonn Era (BE)

Eryndor
Gort da Nair
Pencras
Benvane
Caermor

Sian

MERCENARY & SWORDSWOMAN

Merriment all around and shrouding her. Voices, rumbling on and on over the clutter of dishes and the scattering of sighs— one after the other, closer, farther, closer again yet always announced by sips of cold, thick mead. A fist slammed into a table, and her gaze snapped in its direction. *A happy drunk*, Sian decided, flinching at the man's roaring laughter. Still watching she sucked in a breath, drew in the greasy, heady scent of the tavern: roasted meat mingling with sweat-drenched leather and dried blood—the patrons', all sellswords like her.

Yet her corner was quieter. Far from the hearth, but just warm enough to smother the sweat tickling her nape. One, two drops—as cold and chilling as the mead wetting her ungloved right hand. Sian looked down at it, then at the mug clenched on her fist. *Can't break it; can't pay for anything else.*

Laughter again, roaring even louder. She frowned at the culprit, but his group remained unaware of her annoyance; uncaring, even. It didn't bother her... unlike the two men sitting a couple of tables to her left.

Her comrades. Mewen and Diarmuid.

She'd glanced there before, recognised them all too well. *It can't be.* She glances now again, shifts on her seat to gauge the pair with intent. *But it is they.*

Mewen's blond hair shimmers like his mead, his missing eye

shadowed by unruly brows. He gossips and sinks his forefinger on the table, mocking someone else's speech—and Diarmuid laughs, yellow teeth in display and matching his amber eyes. He grooms his beard, and breadcrumbs scatter onto the table. *They're dead. Why are they here?*

One blink, one sip of her mead—and blood leaks from Diarmuid's mouth, a spear protruding from his chest to stain everything red. So brilliant, that red; so, so— *No. Not here.* She shakes her head, but the tavern is gone and he's splayed on the ground, face up, eyes unseeing, that spear impaling him and never letting him truly rest. *I looted his sword, his pouch.* Shame and sense, because he wouldn't need either anymore while she would.

Another blink and he's talking again, the charred mound on the opposite seat drinking a beer. Mewen, wearing maille dark like cinders, no features, no eyes, no brows, just black char in the shape of a human with a sword nearby. *Could've been him; could've been someone else.* But there are so many in the plains, so many. All charred because the Aelorians dropped fire-pots using their siege machines, and no one survived. *I'm lucky*, she knows it, but shakes her head and feels the cold sweat on her hands. *Lucky because I'm a coward; because I—*

Her teeth grind and she looks down, locking onto the mug on her walnut fist. The mead inside shimmered gold under the torchlight, the sounds of laughter and merriment returning to her lazily. *Fuck!*

One sip, another, another, one more and the mug was empty, lukewarm droplets scattered on her lips. Her tongue darted through them, her thumb rubbing the drinkware's rough wood. *Look up; they won't be here. Haven't been for years.* But her gaze still clung to the mug and the metal cinching it into form. *It's just an echo. Look up!*

The blond man was too young; the bearded one too pale. They were just two more sellswords, alive for now. But not Mewen, not Diarmuid; those two had been long taken by the Spirits.

"Pathetic." Her murmur spilled under a snarl, hidden by

another burst of laughter. *Should've stayed in the farm. Never sign for war.*

Her thumb caught in a wood splinter, and she stifled a whine. She frowned at it, pulled the sting and looked up again—past the tables and the patrons, past the tavern's merriment and into the kitchen's hallway. The barmaid had gone there after taking her coin, and was yet to return. Not with food; the forest would see to that. With supplies. *For my last journey.*

The waiting wore her thin simply because she'd soon recover what she, Mewen, and Diarmuid had long hidden. *A coffer full of jewels and gold.* Long ago they'd buried it near Gort da Nair, and she meant to give it purpose again. *Purchase a homestead. Retire.* She missed the farm where she'd been raised, though she hadn't worked on one in over three decades. *It'd be quiet; without... echoes.* But only if the barmaid—

A body eclipsed the flickering torchlight, pressing a leather scrip onto the table—worn out and patched, but supple like the pale hands holding it in place. A waterskin folded over it, clearly full though she hadn't requested it.

"Bandages, a waterskin..." The barmaid's rough voice was barely audible. She leaned forth, still holding onto the items. A whisper, bare: "And jerky."

Sian looked up, met the woman's tan eyes. "I cannot pay for the jerky."

Yet the addition was welcome. Winter had arrived, scattering the game. *And Gort da Nair is four-weeks away.* The jerky would help.

"On the house." Another whisper—then leather rasped on oak, the scrip and skin stopping before her.

Sian didn't argue and instead pulled the goods close while dipping her head—but the eclipse was gone, the barmaid nowhere to be found. She didn't care, looping both items onto her belt. *Homesteading. Peace.*

Sian exhaled. Her breath fogged near her lips, drifting to join the night's cold. There were patches of warmth under the shafts of torchlight, but the rest was as chalky and iron-grey as the overcast sky.

What an odd town, Pencras. Close to the frontier with the Aelorian inland, but still within Eryndor's steppes; humid and dense in summer, but cold and dry in winter. It was guarded by the northern tip of the Glenbrae, though little it helped—mercenaries always stopped there when near, and so did invaders whenever war approached. *The inns will be crowded tonight,* Sian reckoned, watching the tavern she'd left and the stable nearby. *I could sneak in; sleep on the straw and—*

A horn pierced the night. Wailed and died.

Quiet after, on the streets, in the cold.

Just the bustle of the tavern, muffled by its closed doors. Just the torchlight above her. Just her heartbeat, pounding like a war-drum.

I heard... something? Anything? Tavern. Torchlight. Heartbeats.

Danger prickled at her nape like drops of cold sweat. Tavern. Torchlight. Heartbeats.

The sounds came and went—empty, quiet, empty, quiet. Tavern. Torchlight. Heartbeats.

Her hands found the shortswords on her hips, her feet steered her three steps into the darkness. There she waited, breath held to strangle the fog that could give her away. *Is it an echo?*

Quiet yet, overwhelmed by her heartbeat.

Thump-thump. Thump-thump. Thump-thump.

It rumbled on her fists as she unsheathed her shortswords and glanced left, right, ahead, over her shoulder to see nothing but darkness, nothing but quiet. Sian pressed her lips, steadied her breathing. *The war isn't here... or is it?* Bootfalls chafed in the night, somewhere but moving. Distant, crowded, marching, coming close, looming closer—but soft, so soft. *From the west? Can't be.*

Far away one dot surged onto the chalky sky, westborn and flickering golden. She tracked it with her gaze, but blinked thrice when the chilly breeze dried her eyes. Two more dots joined it, all soaring high, higher, glimmering, growing, arching, plunging, whistling, flames belching from within, ceramic crashing onto rooftops and bursting alight. Red, gold, orange, tongues of warmth and death, licking the wood, searing the breeze, eating her surroundings.

A town, first; wooden-made and simply built. Aflame at nighttime.

A fortress, then; stone-made and ruling a hill. Aflame at daylight.

One isn't real. But which—? Sian breathes pitch-stinking and tar-sweet air, coughs and glances at the stables and the flames corroding the straw. Her eyes water, the breeze throat-scorching as she swallows and stalks closer to it, closer and sees it built from the fortress' wall, closer again but now it's made of wood aflame. *Only one. Which?* Her hand stretches, slow, slower but coveting the fire because if it burned then it'd be proof of her sanity.

Closer, then, closer to—

Silence. Absolute silence.

No tavern noises, no torchlight or flames, not even heart-beats to hammer the silence though she feels it pounding and wrenching her chest. She heaves, forgets the fire, heaves again but something wrings inside her and twists hard, wrenching, tearing, forcing her to stagger—back, back, back and her spine slams against the mouth of an alleyway.

She chokes on the cinder-thick breeze, bile pooling in her mouth, left shortsword slipping from her grip—then catches it mid-air, reverse grip to press her chest and retch because some-thing is tearing it in two.

Yet the silence survives, overpowering.

Within it, one whisper: *'Run to the forest.'*

Yes. Must run. She ought to; she knows it but can't. *The coffer; my homestead.* Can't move, can't breathe, can't—

'Run to the forest.' A whisper amidst silence.

Screams.

From the town, from the houses, from the streets and the forest and the western wall where a horn bellows with an order to charge. An army roars, metal on metal and bootfalls on a sprint running fast, faster, louder.

The pressure eases on her chest. *Look up!* Her attention

snaps, her gaze etches on the shadows swarming the streets. *Must run. To Gort da Nair. Find the coffer.* Sian stumbles, slides back with legs quivering as she staggers and spins, knee hitting the ground, scraping up, stumbling, trotting, running into the darkness and into the forest.

Out of the fortress. Out of the town.

It matters not. She runs east.

MERCENARY & SWORDSWOMAN

Bootfalls, too many, too steady. East to west, marching under the scrape of leather and metal and the crackling of torches. No voices, just muffled murmurs and the booming of distant shouting. No meaning, just noises lurching uphill to infest the forest and find her.

Quiet. Stay quiet. Sian held her breath, stalled it and swallowed hard. *If they aren't here— No. They* are *real. Must be.* Hours had passed though the night endured—but her saliva was still bitter, soot-tainted and dusty. It scraped her throat, itching as she descended through the leaf-covered hillside.

One step, seeking purchase between the fallen leaves.

Another step, pressing into cinder-thick soil.

One more, and her left hand grazed the outcrop's rough side. Her leather gloves rasped on stone, steadying as she dropped to a crouch and took cover. She allowed an idle moment, found her fingers rubbing her sore chest, and hissed. *Just smoke and ash. It'll pass.* But it ached and twisted when she peered over and down the slanted hill.

Soldiers obstructed the road. Columns of them. Dark shapes in the night, crammed into formation. One, two torches only, spaced between them.

Real, then. Sian regarded them, sunk deeper into her crouch and bathed herself in the noise. A march, but not aligned.

Murmurs, but not loud. Metal and leather but dishevelled, unequal. *Sellswords. But whose?* Their march was controlled violence when compared to the forest's life—but not quiet, not silent like Pencras had been. So unnaturally silent. *I was deafened, that's all. I'd drunk too much mead.*

Yet she dallied; kept basking herself in that racket of a march.

Downhill, the soldiers were still marching and murmuring, still dressed in a blend of maille, plate, leathers, anything. *Real.* Relief, though smothered by how many she counted. *A cohort, or maybe two.*

Sian pulled back, retreated behind the rock and stared at the oaks—some barebones, others holding onto coppery canopies. They provided enough cover, but not enough to travel close to the road. *Not with that many soldiers... whoever they are.* Those she'd heard in Pencras had come from the west—from Aeloria— while these marched from Eryndor's inland to clash with the invaders. *Lordling's wars,* she reckoned, tongue darting through the roof of her mouth to clear the bitterness she tasted. She swallowed soot, rested her head on the rock, and looked up.

Above her the sky was a deep tar, patched with chalky clouds and darkening westwards—where a single column of iron smoke soared steadily. *Pencras. A wooden town, not a fortress.* She glanced at the tar, at the clouds, at the forest of rickety canopies. The army's march crept in the stillness. *They're real. They're out there... so I stay in the trees.* A dangerous journey, but the last one she'd take. *To my own homestead.*

The wind shrieked above the distant marching, above her own muffled footsteps. It slithered through the rusty canopies; chilled her sweat like a sharp, deadly blade not yet bloodied.

Sian shivered and looked down, took a few steps and halted again, adjusting her cloak closer to her neck. Her fingertips found the skin between her scalp-braided plaits, rubbed it and came out moist and dusty. The air was heavy, acrid, and smoke- stained—but she resumed marching between the oaks, minding her footfalls although the wind's shrill would certainly hide them.

Two more steps and she scraped the heel of her hand over her leather armour—tracing circles across her chest. On and on as she steered towards a haggard oak, on and on as she moved under the surviving brittle canopies. *This... soot will clear. It was worse after the Siege of Caermor.* It hadn't subsided, that ache she'd caught while escaping Pencras; just eased into a dull throbbing that twisted and tore until saliva pooled in her mouth. *I'm getting old.* She spat it over a leaf, silted and heavy and too acrid—then stepped around, avoided a bush, and looked up.

Above and behind her the sky was a jail of clouds and coal—but ahead, it shone like a forge of blood and liquid gold, strands of bronze and copper burning the remaining clouds. They provided direction, even when she couldn't see the sun itself dawning over the canopies.

Sian allowed herself a smile, walked onwards, surer. *March towards the griadergh, reach Gort da Nair.* It was mesmerising, the Blood of the Sun, the shimmer it poured into the branches, into the—

Darkness. Perfect, unflinching darkness, a few paces ahead. It existed between the oaks, and swallowed the dawn into its black stone.

Sweat tickled down her nape, icy as the breeze hastened again. *A drulock? Plague take me!* Sian watched it, a twitch taking her cheek, her mouth, her jaw. She'd encountered them before—the land seeded them like warnings—and had always taken another way. She didn't believe the legends, but only a fool disregarded the Storytellers' advice. *Move. Steer away. Now!* Her teeth dug into her lips, her heart vaulted to a gallop, but her gaze was etched in the danger ahead.

On that narrow, doorless tower. On the stone, black like coal. On the cloaked silhouette standing atop it—watching her with cerulean eyes brimming under a hood.

Sian stepped back, crushed the fallen leaves on her retreat. *Go back. Around, away.* A chill cleaved through her throat, clawing her neck. *Walk. Move.* One step. One more, again. Again with her fists tight and ready to attack, gaze locked in those cerulean eyes.

Watching. Following. Tracing.

Gone.

One breath, fogging again.

Nothing watching her, nothing after but silence.

Deafening because the leaves didn't rustle, the breeze didn't whistle, the twigs didn't snap when she backtracked again. Just silence and her heartbeat, a war-drum too uneasy to slow down, too hollow to let the world live again. Just silence and that void within her, tensing her jaw, grinding her teeth, knotting her heart until it stuttered into an ill-paced rhythm. *Walk—!*

Sian staggered, left hand flailing and catching a branch. She leaned into it, panted and gagged as saliva flooded her mouth, forcing her to swallow coal—burning down her throat, then creeping up to scorch again. It leaked onto her tongue when dizziness assaulted her, twisting the forest, sending it into a spin. She shut her eyes, shook her head and swallowed again— no blood, no bile, but that iron tang which refused to leave. The spinning hastened, tensed the knot in her heart and pulled, wrenching, tearing, wrenching again.

Nothing in that silence.

Nothing but one whisper: *'They are here.'*

They? Instinct warned her. Danger coiled in her gut, tore again. *The soldiers!* Sian jerked upright.

The forest spun, twisted at the edges, gold light searing her vision.

She blinked, found two soldiers staring at her, at the drulock, at her eyes and the shortswords on her hips. *No, they aren't here. Aren't real.*

But they stare, and she stares back, all quiet and still, all motionless while she blinks and blinks and can't decide. *Real or not?* Instinct tickles cold in her nape; danger wrenches her heart. *Real? Real!?* The forest envelops them all. Half-shadowed and gaunt, shafts of red light pouring in patches because it's too thin to hide any noise, too full of fallen leaves, of twigs to break, of vermin to upset. Too easy to reach if they found her here and she didn't hear them nor see them before.

Nothing yet, but silence. Nothing but one enemy scowling so, so slow that his black brows furrow and furrow while his nose scrunches and his jaw hinges open. *Real or not!?*

She knows the answer, knows it truly.

Hears it whispered: *'Real.'*

A knife pierces one man's eye. He drops to his knees, face down, no movement left.

Sian blinks, sees her hand stretched out and hanging open with fingers half-curled. No knife between them, no knife in her belt either. Just leather rasping leather as she prods it, prods it again, finds the hilt of her shortswords and unsheathes them both.

The other soldier is gone.

Her gaze snaps right, left, half-left, ahead, to the bushes, to her right. She heaves, staggers and looks left, right—

'Dodge.'

Instinct. Danger. Truth.

Sian rolls rightwards and looks up, sees the other man half-hunched and hauling up his sword. He snarls, gaze full of death and murder. The drulock looms behind him, pure black and merely rimmed by the Blood of the Sun—gold, red, flames on that edge, the banner of Death.

He charges, doesn't scream but cleaves. Her shortswords cross, lock his blade and throw it rightwards. She kicks, and he staggers back but hacks again, metal on metal and the sparks that glimmer with the dawn, shrieking, echoing, calling, screaming. *They'll find me.*

One grunt. Hers and her instinct's.

Iron blessed with dawning light, with carmine blood.

Wide eyes on the man. Pale silver, unfocused. Words tumble from his mouth, but red is all that leaks. Red, red, red and silence even as she draws her sword from his chest and kicks him down. He collapses onto the leaves, sends them billowing.

No more silence, just heaving. Hers, and frantic, panting and rasping and spitting saliva because it scorches her throat. No more silence, but voices—asking questions, moving near, slow but close, closer still. *They found me.*

Sian doesn't move. Just gasps and shakes her head, sees the

bodies again, the knife now buried under a corpse. Pick it, leave it, pick it, leave it—she can't decide, can't move, can't think of anything but the noises and the army and the drulock eclipsing the dawn.

'*Escape, fool!*'

Instinct. Danger. Truth.

One step back; it crunches leaves. One more, it shatters a twig. One more, her foot clips the ground, sends her staggering. Her fist presses into a trunk, gives her purchase. *The homestead!* She remembers it now, the homestead and the coffer and her need to reach Gort da Nair—and craves it even more. *Not real, not yet but it will.*

She gags, retching once more. Runs.

Sian

MERCENARY & SWORDSWOMAN

Darkness. Cold, chilling. Black like ink.

Quiet except for that droplet somewhere—tick, tick, ticking into a pool she can't see, can't find, so black it is, so black and dark.

Quiet, but she exhales and breaks the stillness, spins left, right, right again, in circles, in half-circles.

Darkness is all there is.

All about her, all around her.

It looms overhead, reaches with a hand and clenches her heart to wrench harder, twisting, pulling, tearing until she frays into amethyst threads.

Up they go, those violet threads. Up and whispering. Up like her hands, reaching for the one that holds her still—but the threads are gone and so is she, amidst the darkness of the abyss and that tick, tick, tick of water on water.

Sian jerked to a sit and snapped left, right, back and around the cave's gloom. The ragged slashes of her heaving ran within the stone walls, screaming so loud she clasped her mouth and nose to stall the noise. Water dripped somewhere, echoing in a maddening rhythm.

Tick. Tick. Tick.

Like the twitching in her cheek and the cold sweat skidding down her neck. She wiped it in a rush, wiped her temples, her forehead. Her glove was moist again, and the sight of it drove her to shiver.

When she looked up, sunlight blistered the darkness of the cave. She blinked, raised a hand before her eyes, and spread the fingers. Beyond that barrier the light shaped into a crooked oval, buttermilk and soft. *Past noon already?* Thirst assaulted her then, clawing at her throat like the light scratching at her eyes—but Sian did not move, did not breathe and just watched that entrance.

There were no soldiers there, no noises that could give them away either. *Cannot trust it*, Sian knew, and she narrowed her eyes, keened her hearing to search for the army's marching. It didn't come to her, perhaps pacified by the distance and the forest's answer—birds chirping outside, critters scurrying through the bushes.

Stillness, but not silence.

Did I... imagine them? The two men near the drulock? Doubt ate at her, tensed her hand into a fist and released it, tensed it again and couldn't stall the quivering. *Real, or—?* Her other hand found her belt, prodded it back and forth, felt the sheath of her knife and found it empty. She frowned at it. *I threw it... to a soldier? To an animal? To the drulock?*

A grimace curled Sian's lips, reminding her of the thirst. She pulled into a crouch, looked around and saw the shimmer of sunlight on the maddening droplets.

Tick. Tick. Tick.

They kept ringing as she padded towards them, rolling each foot to stay quiet. She stopped near the rocky wall, gnawed her left glove and ripped it off—then pressed her hand into the wetness, tracked it down to a rimstone dam in the ground. The stream within was just two palms wide, but deep enough that she cupped water one-handed and splashed it on her face.

It still echoed when she pulled off the other glove and leaned in, cupping some water to drink, then some more to drench her face, her neck, her hair until the soot stopped itching and only freshness remained. The stream didn't quell but rippled slower and slower while her breathing eased and the walnut outline of her face reflected on the water. It frowned back at her, scrunching its broad nose just like she did. Sian blinked, saw her own pale blue eyes blink—

Darkness. Towering behind her. Lurking closer, reaching for her.

She spun, hand on the hilt of a shortsword. Her breathing halved, heaving fast, faster—silent when she pressed her lips, frowned at the empty, darkened cave. *I'm... half-asleep. Wary of a nightmare's echo.* Shadows were all there was. Shadows, and the faint glow of sunlight rimming the rocky walls. *Getting old as well.*

Yet the feeling lingered, that towering darkness stalking her as she retrieved her gloves and edged closer to the crooked entrance. Her right shoulder pressed into the rough stone, one knee down—though she stayed ready to spring. One heartbeat. She glanced back over her shoulder, scowled at the emptiness behind her. *Just... echoes. The cost of staying alive too long.*

Tick. Tick. Tick.

Maddening.

She snarled. Lingered—yet turned to assess the forest.

The oaks around the cave's entrance were haggard but bore coppery canopies, dimming the noon's honeyed light. Two hares popped out of the bushes, startled at Sian and snapped away. Rustling followed. Rustling, chirping, the breeze, and the forest's stillness. She breathed, glanced back—*Nothing behind me*—then studied the ground outside: grass and leaves in leathery hues, twigs, branches, and no footprints. *Not even mine.* Even in her frantic escape at dawn she'd smeared them whenever possible.

One grunt. Hers, but echoing.

Should leave now, Sian decided, though she didn't unfurl from her crouch. *Travel now and during the night.* She needed to cover as much distance as possible, to move away from that army and a war that didn't pertain to her. *To my homestead, then. First Gort da Nair, then—*

Darkness. It reached for her from the cave, breathed ice down her nape. It stole all sounds.

Silence.

Just silence with droplets that no longer ticked and a breeze that didn't rustle the coppery leaves. Without vermin or crickets, without hooting or chirping.

Just silence, and the march of her heart—dense, steady but fast, faster even, erratic, slashing into a gasp but caught mid-beat by something that twisted and wrenched until Sian dropped to both knees, hands pressed on the rocky ground. She gagged, coughed blades that scraped her throat, then counted the soundless drops leaking from her mouth.

Saliva. One strand, clear. Pulling her chest, twisting her heart.

Bile. Three drops, but acrid and burning her from within. Tightening that pressure until she hacked, dry and acrid.

Blood. Clotted, carmine and thick because something was tearing her apart, wrenching her in half while she couldn't swallow, couldn't spit, couldn't breathe. Just choke without air, just heave and lick her broken lips.

It yanked, that pressure on his chest. Wrung and wrenched until Sian buckled forward and tore open her jaw, screaming in guttural silence. Her hands clutched the rocks, quivered and faltered but steadied before the ground scraped her chin. Warmth twisted in her chest. Cold chilled her neck, her cheeks, the sweat dotting the scalp between her braids.

She felt it, then. The shadow towering behind her.

It sighed. Like a woman; a veteran.

Whispered, half-burnt and exhausted: *'Fear? Why?'*

Fear held her fast. Tensed Sian's neck as she turned, slow, heavy, but more and more and more.

The cave was half-dark half-lit. Empty and silent.

No soldiers. Nothing. But she didn't sigh; had no relief. *No one followed me. No...* A frown tensed her face, wrung her heart again. Sian shook her head, wrestled against that force to hoist one knee up and plant the foot. *Just a nightmare's echo. Mewen's echo.* She lifted a hand to the wall, scraped at the roughness, loosened pebbles and clawed again, seeking purchase. *He...*

always asked that, yes. Her fingers clenched hard when she hauled herself to a stand—then staggered forth until her hands braced her knees, all limbs quivering like the leaves of the rickety oaks. *Why fear? He asked that. I ask it now.*

A smile eased her grimace. Allowed some relief.

He saved me once with that question. She knew it, remembered it while resting a hand atop the hilt of a shortsword, the other across her chest. *He saves me again.* The pain was quelling and fading, perhaps never there. Another sigh, then she turned fully towards the cave.

Empty. Just shadows broken by shafts of sunlight. Just shadows and that maddening drip.

Tick. Tick. Tick.

Yet it watched her, that empty cave. It watched her and moved closer, closer still as Sian staggered into the forest and trudged away.

A waking nightmare; that's all. Sian halted, pressed one hand into a tree, the other under her ribs, massaging. The wrenching force had reduced to an annoyance lodged in her chest. *Diarmuid had them, yes. Waking nightmares. Awful things.* Cold sweat prickled the base of her neck, but she didn't rearrange her cloak; left it crooked as she looked up to the sky—brassy, bleeding anew— then over her shoulder and back.

Nothing had followed her; no one towered near. *I'd just woken up. Seeing Mewen in that tavern summoned the nightmares.* But there'd been shadows in that cave. A woman with a question.

Mewen's question made mine. But it was no excuse; she knew it. Three decades of war had taught her what happened to those who lowered their guard; those who let the echoes hound them. *More reasons to retire. Purchase that homestead.* She pressed her lips, butchered a grunt and regarded the forest beyond her.

Lonely. Quiet, but alive.

Leaves rustled in the cool wafts. Vermin scurried through the shrubs. An owl hooted from the nearest canopy.

Can't hear the army. She sealed her lips, listened intently while staring at the gaunt oaks. Wood screeched in the distance; horses perhaps neighed and trotted over crushed dirt. *Supplies? A new watch?* The noises faded too quickly—but the unease lingered, lurking. *Fool. I can take a few soldiers.* Yet the last two—

Sian stalled the hand rubbing her chest, lowered it and prodded the empty knife sheath on her belt. *Those two, real. The cave... a waking nightmare. Gone, now.*

Her lips curled between a grimace and a snarl, lingering half-shaped while she distrusted the forest. *Eastwards, then. To Gort da Nair.*

The sky was a shield of pitch darkness and soot, yet it bled westbound with the hues of Death—with tongues of red, as brilliant as fresh blood, and clots of crimson and carmine splotched over swirls of gold. The nefrudh, the Red Heavens, dusked and died so slowly it soaked the canopies above her with gore. Just traces in the edges of leaves and branches—but deep and dark and too reminiscent of a battlefield.

Sian grimaced at it but trudged on, shivering when the breeze chilled her neck. She tugged at her cloak, clutched it one-handed while the other rubbed her chest—sore and worn after twisting and twisting without respite. *I need to rest. In an inn.* Her heartbeats were as ragged as her march. *Or somewhere without nightmares. That'd be enough, yes.* She hiked eastwards with throbbing legs, each step stuttering on her tense calves and ricocheting up her knees. *Stretch, perhaps. Diarmuid always insisted.* He used to—

Darkness. Ebbing.

Her breath hitched. She kept trudging, forgetting her footing —but peered back. Frowned.

The forest was quiet and lonely, darkening as the nefrudh died.

Twilight. Tricky thing. With vermin and critters and leaves rustling and crinkling—but nothing else. No footsteps save hers, no words save her thoughts. The wagons she'd heard earlier that day had long perished into the distance, the army's march gone since she'd run from the drulock. *Another waking—*

Darkness towered over her.

It breathed ice down her neck.

Sian halted, waited for her own noises to die, then glanced over her shoulder. *No soldiers, no animals, nothing.* Just leaves and branches coated in the bloodied light of the Red Heavens. *Just the nefrudh teasing my eyes.*

Idly, she fished her belt scrip for some jerky and munched twice before resuming her trudge. *Find the coffer, purchase a homestead. Retire.* The salt stung her parched lips, but she gnawed hard, harder to tear a bite. Her chewing deafened her; left a greasy, smoke-scented taste in her mouth. She savoured it while peering back again.

Through the right shoulder, the left, the left again, forward for three steps and another glance while she chewed. *Nothing follows me; just shadows.* Her scrip thudded as she folded the flap and thumbed it over the stud—but her hand lingered there, edging closer to the hilt of a shortsword. *The echoes of yore tease me again. Can't let them. Must find that coffer.* The weight of her hand muffled the faint clack of the sheaths, letting her focus on—

Darkness. Eating the bleeding light, staining it pitch black.

Sian cut her stride. Gripped her hilts and turned around fully.

Nothing but the forest. It waited for her, all shadows and blood and gold. *Not real.* She jammed her hands into her browbone, shut the eyes and shook the head. Left and right. Left and right. Looked up, blinked at the forest anew.

No hint of life, no game sneaking through shrubs, no birds hooting in the canopies. No one following, not even after she blinked and squinted at the oaks.

Nothing but that darkness standing beside her.

Just light and nightmares. Not real, no. Hands pressed her browbone. Hard. Head left, right, left, right. Looked up. Blinked. Coughed the tension twisting her chest. *Ash, soot. Age. The homestead will help.*

Brow. Pressure. Shake. Left. Right.

Up.

Blink.

Just fear. Like Mewen said.

Hands. Brow.

Left. Right.

Up.

Cold skittered icy between the tight rows of her braids, down her neck, down her shoulders and down again. It summoned a shiver, slithered unheard and wiped out all sounds.

Silence drowned her. Offered one whisper: *'Fear is the enemy.'*

Nothing. Just her own thoughts.

Mewen said that. Many times, yes. Sian remembered him stating it, on and on before each battle, before the enemies charged towards them or before themselves faced Death. *Fear is the enemy.* She'd whispered it herself two heartbeats ago. Knew how it continued, that warning. *Fear kills. Twists the mind.*

Still she backtracked one step, two steps, one more, another, another, two, three, half-turning and stopping again, clawing at the air, snatching for purchase and stumbling forth.

Her hands braced her weakened knees, quivered and threatened to crumble. The ground beneath spun, slow and lazy but round and round and round again until saliva pooled under her tongue. Sian gagged, retched the acid creeping and burning from within.

Droplets hit the ground—thin, clear beads pooling between her feet like counters of failure. Each dripped without noise, with just colour topping more colours. Silent and—

'Fear walks you to the grave.'

"Yes!" Sian heaved. Spat clear, yellow, red—then rubbed her chest through her leathers. "I said… it. To M-mewen."

She says it again, hidden behind birches on the eve of a summer ambush. *Fear walks you to the grave,* she hisses and cocks a brow. He stifles a laugh, bites his tongue, and nods to her. *No; he's dead.* But he's there, back slammed against a tree, sword on hand and rolling two fingers because she's dallying and he's demanding. She chuckles and chokes, sucks in humid air, cold air, sees the birches, sees the oaks, hears herself answering him once more.

'It digs the hole and tucks you in.' A whisper, but her lips don't move, just quiver.

He grins, broken teeth on display. One nod, and he hoists his sword. *Fear is how we die,* he answers or perhaps she thinks it loudly, but it matters not because they charge and her heart leaps and stutters, tumbling, twisting, stilling, tumbling again, erasing the birches, recalling the oaks, no daylight all nighttime, no summer all winter, all darkness and shadows and her heartbeats with no rhythm just a sequence awry with no mercy, no peace, no surrender to that wrenching force that pulls and pulls and pulls until she blinks and black splotches the nascent night.

Darkness.

Without it, nothing. Within it, strands.

Amethyst strands. Curling like smoke.

Streaming from her chest.

Sian gagged, scraped at her neck, gasped and gagged again—but her heart writhed, that smoke twisting and twining, over and over to wring and wring and wring. Her lips quavered. Shaped a grimace, a snarl, a howl. Her fingers twitched and snapped but seized nothing because the smoke soared between them, violet and violent and shaped like strings.

It yanked at her, dropped her into the ground.

Stone waited for her under the leaves. Scraped her. Scraped her again until blood warmed her forehead and it itched and burnt and ignited the tension in her chest.

Look... up! But she couldn't move her limbs, couldn't will them to push her back to her feet—just stare at the amethyst smoke, just breathe and feel the blood in her forehead, lick the one in her lips. Metallic, tangy, dirt-ridden and thick like bile. *Look up. To the night.* She begged herself, watched the smoke, and licked her lips again. Made that taste all there was. *Look up. It's not real, just a waking night—*

"Yes. Look up." A whisper.

Her eyes snapped. Cut through the shadows close, far, close, closer, violet, smoke, far, amethyst, far, farther, on, on, on—

A shadow.

Crouching at the other end of the amethyst smoke. Woven from darkness and shaped like a woman with shortswords at her hips. It cocked its eyeless head, scrunched a broad nose before offering a snarl.

Sian blinked; she remembered that gesture. Had seen it before, almost every day.

Did it as the darkness took her.

Sian

MERCENARY & SWORDSWOMAN

Nighttime. Black splotching on black wherever she looked. Crooked half-moons blazing opalescent over it. Blinding all details with white, pink, purple.

"Look up." She whispered it. Came exactly as she'd heard it. "Look up."

The forest; passing by as she trudged. Black on black, but opalescent in arcs. White, pink, purple.

No shadows; no woman. Just my eyes. She blinked again, massaged her temples, and lumbered on. Felt her lower lids twitching, twitching, twitching to make it all shine brighter. *Breathe. Kill your fear.* She'd said that to Mewen once, when he got that cut across his right eye and lost it.

"Breathe. Keep looking up." Her whisper, her words over the racket of her sore heart, over her ragged footsteps. *Like before. Like always.*

Nothing else. Not even the fear she'd questioned sometime ago.

She kept plodding. *To Gort da Nair. To the coffer.*

Shadows near the trees. Shaped like decrepit branches, not like fingers reaching for her as she moved. Not like a woman woven from darkness. Not rimmed in amethyst smoke either.

Stop imagining shapes, she told herself. Grimaced but lumbered on, one hand across her chest. *Fear kills. Twists the mind.*

Cold sweat. Breath hitched, fogged.

Sight cleaved by opalescent half-moons: white, pink, purple. Searing the forest, fading too slowly. *What if I'm... being followed? Truly?* Her heartbeat stumbled, tripped, restored a march—skewed and tough.

Like her steps, eastbound. *To my homestead.* Repeated beside her.

Her cheek twitched.

Repeated? The half-moons tracked her sight as she looked back, blazed and burnt brighter. Ahead. Back. Right. Left. Left!

A shadow followed her. A woman woven of darkness.

Sian pursed her lips and butchered a gasp. *Could be real, could be not.* But the shadow-woman... moved through the ground fog of amethyst coils and mimicked Sian's pace. Teased a memory she buried again.

No, no. She blinked, kept walking and rubbed an eye. The half-moons softened, lingered, blazed back. White, pink, purple, all colours twisted. *Too silent; too careful. Must be the night's deed.* It had to be. No one walked in absolute silence. No one became one with the shadows. *Not real, then; just my fear. It teases me.* Just the fear and her exhaustion. Just a trick of her eyes and the forest and the night and the moonlight hidden beyond chalky clouds. *Should find somewhere to sleep. To hide and lure whoever follows me... if real.* She looked around; saw nothing but trees and shadows and shrubs and that woman of darkness with swords at her hips. *Can't afford more nightmares. Can't afford... being followed to my coffer and my homestead.*

An icy breeze, chilling because her cloak dragged over one shoulder and not the other. She pulled it straight, covered her neck. Frowned at its amethyst rim, frayed into strands—billowing towards the shadow. *Just light-tricks. Just—*

"Breathe."

Her whisper, surely. Hers only.

I was wrong. Someone found me. A woman, Sian guessed, swordfighter like herself. A soldier from the army marching to Pencras, or a friend of the two she'd killed. She was covert, walking through the ground fog to appear like a shadow mound. *But she's there; I see her. She's real. I was wrong.* Only the coils of amethyst smoke gave her away. It bled from her, surrounded her. *The moonlight's reflection. The Spirits aid me.* Silent otherwise, that woman; that enemy. So silent even the forest had forgotten its own noises.

Only her heartbeat survived—pounding, pounding, pounding relentless and erratic, stumbling whenever the tension within her wrenched tighter, wrenched some more. Sian lifted a hand. Pressed it under her ribs and massaged right, left, right, left. Her gaze followed, searching the forest's darkness. Right, left, right, left. *There!*

The shadow. That woman.

Moving eastbound, legs hidden in the ground fog. Head up.

Must be real. But why hasn't she attacked? Sian glanced at her, prodded her leathers down to her belt, past the empty knife sheath, and to the waterskin. She thumbed it loose, pulled it up and ripped the cork free with her teeth; it rasped her gums, but she spat it into her hand and lifted the skin. *Is she... a recruiter? Has orders not to kill me?* The water soothed her throat, also fresh on her parched lips. She licked them, coveting each droplet—then corked the skin and looped it through her belt, plodded ahead still massaging her twisted chest. *Not real, maybe. Not real and just my tired eyes.* But Sian remembered what she'd seen during the nefrudh, the certainty that someone had been there. *Perhaps I was wrong. I have been before... and may be so now.* The hours after, when she'd been alert and so sure no one had followed her. *It could've been fear. Mewen said fear—*

"Fear corrodes. It gnaws at you."

Sian clasped her mouth and nose, clenched hard. Hard enough her blunt nails sank into her cheeks. *Why did I speak? Why?* She'd repeated what Mewen had said, her own voice so clear she grimaced behind her curled fingers, hissed a curse and didn't let go. *Fool of me.* Fatigue was affecting her. *Haven't slept properly since before Pencras; drank little, ate less.* But there was no time to hunt game either, not with that shadow-woman stalking her, not with the ground fog and the amethyst smoke warning her. *Should hide, then. But where?* She hadn't discovered any other cave, not even a copse with enough trees to ambush whoever followed her. *But whose banner is she under?* Sian stole another glance. There were no colours on the woman, no arm-wrap disclosing whose gold had her loyalty.

"Listen—"

Sian's voice, surely. Hers or her thoughts because she'd considered them so intently she'd heard them like a voice. *Or not real at all.* Her lids twitched. Twitched again, drew her cheek taut. Once, twice, thrice like a mirror of her steps. *One way to know. Real or not.*

She jerked to a halt. Pursed her lips, knitted her brows tightly—then listened.

To the forest in its shearing silence.

To the game and vermin in their absence.

To the army that no longer marched and the wagons too far away.

To her heart, drumming fast, faster yet, tense and fast, fast, fast and wrenched apart, tore in half and given away—but pounding loud, louder even, louder yet until that was all she heard, all she felt.

Thump-thump thump-thump thump-thump.

Twisting. Tearing. Wrenching.

Not real. Not real. The half-moons returned, searing, blazing. Sneaked wherever Sian looked, flared brighter when she gasped and clutched her chest—though the arcs tarnished the forest, the ground fog, the amethyst coils and the woman standing before her.

The woman.

Close.

Shadow-woven like night itself, the shape of her body so smeared her armour had no details, no clarity. *Who is she?* Full lips, broad nose; grimly set, both of them. *Like mine.* Thick brows, also; scowling—but no eyes under, nothing there, not even scars.

Her lips curled into a snarl. Twisted Sian's heart. Whispered in her voice: "Would you listen?"

"Would you listen?" Sian uttered. Carefully. Louder, then. "Would you listen?"

She did. Jammed a fist into her swollen chest, clasped the other over it and listened hard. *It's silent. I'm alone.* Both hands kneaded across her ribs to soothe the wrenching force while she listened again.

Nothing in that silence absolute.

Nothing but her torn heartbeat hammering like a war-drum and the rasping of leather on leather: her gloved hand rubbing back and forth, back and forth, kneading and kneading and marking a pattern. It mingled with the drumming, crafted a rhythm that smothered all noises to wipe them clean and silent.

Thump-thump, thump-thump, thump-thump.

No one spoke but me. Sian had blurted a question; that'd been all. *Three times, yes.* It'd been shock, thirst, hunger, lack of sleep. *Fear. It kills; twists the mind. Like Mewen said.*

Realisation, merciful realisation. *It's just fear. Not real.* Soothing the tension, softening that wrench. *The voice, not real.*

"No. Don't—!"

Sian had said it. Blurted it again. *Should still my tongue. Keep my words to bargain for my homestead.* A smile eased her lips, curled her eyes while she looked left, looked right, ahead.

There was darkness before her. A mound of shadows in the shape of a swordswoman with full lips, a broad nose, and a frown Sian knew too well. The half-moons in her eyes made the darkness shimmer violet, coiling, twisting weaker and weaker. *The moonlight's tricks. Like the Storytellers warn. Nothing more.* It was just the light, just her exhaustion—but they conspired with the forest and teased her. Formed shadows from the night because fear ruled her and it twisted the mind. *Won't let it. Have a coffer to unearth.* A smile eased her lips, quelled the twisting force within her. *The shadow, not real.*

"No! Here! See—!"

Nothing to see but the night. Sian's eyes cut through the forest, past the shadow she'd imagined as a woman—but the half-moons chased her gaze, opalescent, shimmering, blinding, bursting white-pink-purple to erase that mound, to blur it, to smear it, to make it nothing while her heartbeat tore again, tore and tore but faded and faded and lessened the pain, scattered the smoke as well. *The smoke, not real.*

"No! Wait—!"

Whispers in the breeze. Chilling, quiet, prickling her neck even as Sian stepped back, pressed her spine against an oak and basked on the coldness bouncing from silence to stillness to silence again. Darkness coming and going, silver, amethyst, silver, amethyst, black like ink splotching through her sight at the rhythm of her slurring heart.

Thump, thump. Thump, thump.

"Why..." Her voice, perhaps. It had to be. Weak; tired, like her. "Why c-can't you... accept us?"

Sian frowned. Watched the darkness not blurred by the moonlight, the shapeless mound that still lingered before her. *Not real.*

Her heart stumbled. Twisted, plunged, hopped again, tumbled, settled. She gaped, tried to form her answer—*Know it, just say it*—but the words dragged through her tongue, through the dusty, acrid saliva, through the scorch creeping through her throat. *Say it,* Sian demanded of herself, jammed her fists into her chest and tried again.

"There is..." Heavy words, thick as well. Rolling on her mouth, leaking with her saliva and blood. "—no 'us.' Just me."

A woman shrilled. It ripped the black open and restored all sounds. It flooded the forest with life and death and darkness and moonlight and the colours that washed away to—

Amok

SOUL TRANSMUTER ALCHEMIST. THE UNTAMED ONE

Midnight poured into the forest, drowning the oaks and casting shafts of darkness the moonlight never defiled. It cleansed the oaks of their harshness, smoothed the gnarled branches and thickened the canopies—yet it avoided the face of the woman dead at the foot of one trunk.

Amok recognised what had driven her. The pervasive need to diminish the vast unknown into a known fact, no matter how reductive and ill-fitting—another trait innate to humankind. They speculated about the Uncharted throughout their fleeting lives, yet sought to annihilate its fullness by reducing ambiguity and uncertainty into incomplete principles—regardless of whether they encompassed the complexity that so troubled them. Since the elder times, humans had let their simplified narratives shape their perception, their interactions, and their evolution in a futile attempt to impose order and coherence upon a universe that would always exceed them.

Yet in that bleak darkness with no dawn or dusk, Amok suspended their indignation to invite what humans refused so intently: curiosity.

They hovered down from between the canopies until their feet grazed the fallen leaves, their ensuing footfalls silent because they so willed it. Their cloak of liquid ink billowed in the breeze, leaking blackness and shimmering glyphs that swarmed around them as they approached the body.

The subject had collapsed lifeless, her body prone on the ground with her back against an oak and legs splayed. Her hands remained near her chest, trapped by the friction of leather on leather, her head tilted back and left—locked in a perennial howl, pale blue eyes open and unseeing.

A look of ultimate torment, of agony equivalent to the most harrowing suicide any human could undertake. An unexpected result, but an illuminating one—another impulse the alchemist had allowed due to their Naturalist alignment... and solely because of what it may reveal.

As the Untamed One observed her, three glyphs soared from between the folds of their cloak to stop between them and the subject—offering their records for further perusal.

Teased by curiosity, Amok slid a hand through the one flickering onyx—their first theory, posed at the onset of the experiment and later rejected. Erroneously, they'd considered the subject's actions to be a form of denial, when such a response was infeasible—for someone, either alchemist or human, could neither extricate themselves from their own existence, nor negate the core of their being.

Thus, they allowed that glyph to rejoin the others before collecting a jade-shimmering one—their second theory, now proven. The subject had killed her *self* by reducing a part of it— the embodiment of the alive elements Amok had attempted to incarnate—into limited facts. After all, someone's interpretation of their own experience was not idle commentary but an intrinsic aspect of it... and by stripping nuance and flattening meaning, she'd instigated something not too unlike the mutilation of the self. As a result, the incarnated Shadow had vanished to—

A last glyph interrupted them, drifting airborne and replacing the jade one over Amok's open palm. It blazed ruby and gold, and it teased the alchemist with a new question—one encountered as the result of the experiment and, if pursued, promising comprehension of a shard of the Uncharted: could such self-mutilation be induced?

Disgust darkened the ink leaking from the Untamed One's cloak, sickening the ruby glyph until it shivered, dense and murky and stained from within. They jailed it between their clenched fingers, consuming its light and locking it in the galaxy swirling within them.

Sheer folly, to allow such a question to roam freely and be pursued by non-Naturalist alchemists—those that'd eagerly spend all humans, all sources of alive elements, in answering it. Sheer folly, not to act in the best interests of Soul Alchemy.

The breeze soared at that instant, rustling the canopies but never allowing the moonlight to breach the darkness of that forest. It was absolute and impermeable, black and abyssal like the ink of the Untamed One's cloak—and it lashed in the night, scattering some glyphs that promptly reassembled to present the alchemist with a linked pair: one jade, one cyan, a theory partly solved, partly unsolved.

Curiosity flared within the Untamed One, dulling their aggravation until they plucked the pair airborne. Its question stemmed from the subject's method of suicide: why had her pain subsided?

It was a nuanced inquiry, given that Amok's process to incarnate thoughts, emotions, and attitudes—alive elements all —was unavoidably painful. It required sundering the self to stream it into a vessel, the Shadow, and ensure its autonomy— an unravelling achieved through the amethyst Strands. A process that, for all their efforts, remained... disturbingly stochastic.

Still the alchemist grinned, and the gesture slashed their non-face, revealing the abyss within. It craved knowledge, it sought to chart the Uncharted and revelled in the fragment now shimmering jade—part of the linked pair, the answer to the question.

The subject's method of suicide had thinned the part of *her* streamed through the Strands into the most absolute minimum —and in the process, the incarnate's intangible pain had become so absolute, so overwhelming and unassailable that her mind had simply disavowed it. Her response had hastened the thinning, leaving the Shadow incomplete.

A complex suicide, unseen in the history of Soul Alchemy, and one perhaps worthy of Amok's next research—undertaken, perhaps, after they finally perfected the incarnate soul-skill.

Yet as they basked in that possibility, another glyph drifted forth—blazing red and gold like the dawns of Nuu to offer a question and promise another shard of the Uncharted. Amok knew what that question was; they'd pondered it since the beginning of the experiment: what alive elements had they precisely incarnated?

The answer still eluded them. Teased them with theories they could neither prove nor disprove.

Amidst the silence of that abyssal midnight and under the cover of its darkness, the Untamed One watched the corpse at the foot of the trunk, her profile warmed by the light of that ruby glyph. Amok's original target had been her self-imposed demands—common in warriors like her, forced to exist at the limit of coherence just to ensure survival. Yet that incarnation had... degenerated. Morphed on its own to first incorporate a desire to be acknowledged—not too dissimilar to hers—and then manifest the fear of demise.

"Desire to exist, fear to cease..." Amok's voice slithered through the night, quiet and powerful, yet heard by none other than them. It answered the first inquiry with another, for a true solution did not yet exist. "Can the Shadows... draw the primal states every being has? Fear, and desire?"

A new pursuit of knowledge, and one that glided through the night, soundwaves morphing into shapes to craft another glyph and stain it ruby-gold. An opportunity like no other, yet a future one—perhaps to be tackled after the incarnate had been finally mastered.

Satisfied with the outcome, the Untamed One rolled two fingers, and their glyphs soared alongside them—rejoining the ink of their cloak. It'd been a most productive experiment, Naturalist in design and outcome, and richer than expected.

A partial success, since this subject had tolerated the incarnate's Strands enough for the Shadow to form... but a failure for she'd lacked the needed curiosity, instead being too predisposed to escape and thin—a flaw that had, in turn, limited her ability to accept her situation, leading to her demise. Lessons learnt, then, and all to be applied during the selection of the following subjects.

After all, Amok's research could only end when proven or disproven—and neither had happened. Yet.

Chapter 3

Corvalen Caelands

1473 Bonn Era (BE)

CORVALEN
GLEAN MÓR
TIDNEMED
TEIFI
DUNLOW
FIDRUAD
VELBRAN
N

Cellach

CHIEF, DUNLOW WESTERN WARRIORS

Gold-edged claws ripped the afternoon's bronze sky to spill pathways of blood and rivulets of night. *The Red Heavens.* Cellach frowned at the nefrudh, tracing its westbound light as it dusked over the canopies—oozing a pungent earthy scent, but gloomy and full of needles. *Like the Aelorian's blades; stained black.* A grunt escaped him, tightening his scowl as he turned north-east, gaze etched high above. *Still hours until night,* though a few stars twinkled already, a trio shimmering silver. *Artanem's claw?* If so, he hadn't lost his path after crossing the Teifi's northern shore while blindfolded by mist. *The Spirits guide me. Even after what I did...* It'd be a matter of following the sky-bear's path: without rest, without hesitation. *Returning to Gleann Mór for a third time, to—*

His throat twisted, stole a grunt from him.

When he looked down, the nefrudh's bloody light pooled near his boots, stretching the shadow of half a man.

Maimed. Less.

Him.

"Move." Growled, low.

Yet he waited, chewed his saliva until his gaze detached from that shape—then sneaked through the darkened blades of grass and into the pinecones scattered to his left. Some were pitch-black, others maroon like crusted blood... but all shimmered amethyst, blurred under that unusual smoke.

It'd been there for a month or so, that amethyst fog-smoke. Around him. Always around him.

Trace it. He commanded it of himself—but when his eyes clenched shut, he sighed and begged instead. *Mind-rot, a curse, a sign of the Spirits. Whatever it is. Trace it.* A stone lodged in his throat at the mere idea, jamming his breathing until his heart hammered unsteadily like a drunken blacksmith. *Look left!* His eyes snapped open, charting the shimmer across the grass, back to his feet, around him, towards his right and into the humanoid mound of darkness standing under a red-barked pine.

A warrior, or the silhouette of one, shadow-woven and half-turned away from him. It wore a sword on its left hip, but everything else was indistinguishable.

It didn't have the sword before! Or perhaps it had... perhaps it had not. No way of knowing. What Cellach remembered... was uncertain, fragmented. Rotting with the nightmares that twisted reality until every waking moment rippled with the echoes of yore. *More reasons to return to Gleann Mór and stay there.*

That drunken blacksmith of Cellach's heart dropped its hammer, pounding once and into absolute silence. It'd grown fuller since the shadow had appeared, becoming too large for himself yet somehow empty and halved—so he pressed a fist into his chest, massaged circles with the futile hope his heart would find its rhythm again. *Breathe.*

Hitched, rattled. *Breathe!*

Easing.

Cellach risked another glance. *But what is that shadow?* The answer had been the same since he'd departed Dunlow: mind-rot, a curse, or a sign of the Spirits. *Not the latter, no. I'm not worthy, just... rotting from inside.* He looked away from that humanoid mound and into the pines ahead.

"Move."

This time his legs obeyed his command, but one knee almost buckled with the first step and the other shook when his weight shifted. He snarled but kept upright, clenching his jaw and enduring the ache—for one breath, no more, and then he trudged again, slipping between shrubs and bushes twitching with game. *Twelve days of marching since leaving Dunlow... and I'm already tired. Pathetic.*

A howl. Wailing agony or deranged laughter tumbling from the treetops.

Cellach pivoted on his heel, right side opening, hand falling onto the hilt of his sword. *The shadow? Where is it?* Nowhere he looked. Not right, not left, just gone—like the amethyst smoke. Gone. *Where!?* Right, right again, left, ahead, right and scowling at the Fidnemed then over one shoulder, over the other. *Where!?* But his heart was out of control, hammering on his neck, on his temples, on his wrist and dulling his sight until the night crept inward—dark, darker. *Focus!* Pines, red-barked. Bushes, mushrooms, the twisted silver light of the moon. Leaves rustling. Movement on his left. *There!*

A hare twisted mid-leap and darted under a shrub.

Cellach hissed, still low in a fighter's crouch... and waited. Waited. Waited and glanced at the shadows at his feet—*No fog-smoke, no violet, no amethyst*—around the bushes, beneath the canopies and broken by the moonlight and the breeze knifing icy through his jaw. *Was it even real? How much... have I rotted?* He couldn't know, just guess and purse his lips to seal the wariness within him. *Perhaps—*

The howl returned, guttural and mangled into half-shaped words—then soared amidst the rustle of wings, sailing into the sky.

A raven. It must be. But he didn't believe himself, didn't lower his guard—just advanced one step, one more, cracked a twig with the third but took another, then two. *Keep moving.* His heart rang in his ears whenever his gaze darted around, but it found nothing. He was alone.

Away from the shadow and its wake of amethyst smoke.

Away from his pursuers.

Keep moving. Can't stop until morning, or they'll find me.

Every muscle, every joint, even his heart. Sore. Aching and refusing any movement, any rhythm.

Cellach worked his jaw, tasting the saliva in his mouth—not enough to quench his thirst, to stop his hand from lodging on the waterskin at his belt. *Fool, I drank at midnight. Hold!* That long, unwanted and enforced stay at Dunlow had dulled his edge, taught him to crave what he'd never needed before. *Useless half-man. Should've left sooner; long before the shadow—* He snarled and forced his hand away from the liquid relief, etching his gaze on a red-barked pine.

"Move." Hissing, but barren like his mouth. "Move!"

His legs refused him; threatened to buckle. A snarl contorted his mouth, building a growl—

Danger tickled cold down his shoulders, slipping into him. Wrenching.

Cellach spun left, chasing the darkness at the corner of his sight—but his foot shaved the ground and he staggered back, unbalanced. The forest reeled past him—bark, bushes, pines, shreds of dawn, shafts of shade, shrubs, vermin, fog-smoke, branches. He stretched without thinking, left arm reaching for the nearest trunk—close, close and so far away—but it slipped out of his grasp and he plunged, unstoppable.

The ground slammed his back, tearing a growl from his throat and unleashing his hammering heart. Brash, distorted. Churning the edges of his vision until all he saw was the Blood of the Sun.

The dawn. Red. So red.

No.

Red everywhere.

No, no, no...

Hues of red, in bright rivulets or matted like clotted blood streaked with sinew. Pouring from the sky's coal-copper shield and half-blinded by the treetops, half-eclipsed by the shape of his arms—stretching up, reaching high. Whole, the right one; clad in leather, wrapped in a vambrace, a bare sunkissed hand. Halved, the left one; cut past his elbow and lighter although he could feel the weight of his hand, stretch the fingers, fist them again.

Hold a shield overhead.

Not of copper but wooden-made, iron-rimmed and heavy, heavier by the moment, heavier as he heaves because the arrows drum against it and threaten his hold. Loud and raucous, a storm without rhythm but full of death, full of screeching as the wood tears open, light screaming and blinding, ivory and bloody and blighting the battlefield beyond: all chaos and mayhem but deafened by their thudding, by the war, by the name he roars.

"Sláine!" Rumbling on his throat, muffled by the screams. "Sláine, here!!"

But she doesn't come and the arrows keep plunging, keep drumming and dragging his shield down and down and down. One arrow whistles past the rim, another sinks at his feet—and Cellach growls, clenches his left hand and angles the shield again, less, more, more and under the rumbling of iron, down and up, down. *Hold!* Steadying himself, he glances at his right arm, at the sword in his hand, at the blond man at his feet. Scrabbling on hands and knees, head bloodied and floundering without sense but still alive, still breathing. *The Spirits show mercy.*

"Murchaud!" Howled. Deafened. *Spirits, please...* "Stand up! It's an order!"

Murchaud grunts, shakes his head and mumbles something —but Cellach can't hear, can't move either, can't haul him onto his shoulder and retreat because the arrows will pierce them, kill them. He snarls, clenches his jaw and—

A scream pierces the mayhem like Death charging at them.

Bellowing like the arrows still plunging down, sibilant and closing fast, one drilling into his shield, another tearing a splinter and letting him see—past the blight of light and into the battlefield and the yelling Aelorian rushing at him with an axe overhead.

Dodge! He stays. Parries the first blow with his shield, hears the screeching of wood, the growl of his enemy and then his own, Murchaud's, someone's, arrows hissing, splinters falling, leather rustling, something buzzing in his ear, pounding in his chest and amidst it all the shimmer of light in his sword—lifting high, higher, aiming, thrusting—

Nothing.

No time. No motion.

Just the wood shattering and the blackened axe hauled up from his forearm. Just the chalky, jagged spikes protruding from it. Just red all over and a hand crashing onto his face, fingers sluggish when he curls them. Strings, as well. Slick and glossy and spilling from the crooked forearm—half-torn but half-there, his and not his and broken like the remains of the shield.

Another scream, wailing, less muffled, volleying from him and wrong, so wrong and absent but present because his hand is sliding down his face though his arm is up and ready to parry—present and gone, present and gone and hollow and weightless but maimed and heavy and light. Dead, not dead, numb, alive, burning while everything else is cold, colder, clammier, iron-thick and roaring in silence, darkness buzzing inwards and fast until all he sees is the Aelorian tumbling sideways while Cellach himself plunges into an abyss.

An arm slips under him and hauls him, yanks him into a sprint, his legs tangling then dragging, trying to move, to step, to run—but he can't, can't stand, can barely breathe. He blinks, light-drunk and giddy and slow because the ground is flowing fast and his left arm is dangling half-torn. Swinging, swinging—

Growling, beside him. A woman's. "Chief! Look up!"

He does. Slow. Slowly up, up, up to Sláine's profile—snarling and baring her teeth, frowning with hatred, with worry, with sweaty black hair stuck on her face and more sounds in her mouth.

Sounds, so many of them, so little about them.

Hailing all over and mingling with colours, with scents, with everything. Soldiers charging, metal chafing, banners burning, sweat and musk and pungent corpses, earth and broken arrows, shouting, horns—*Retreat? I'd ordered it, yes...*—leather boots, the ground beneath, trees, grass and blood and trunks and the world tumbling and slamming against his back. The sky. Soft ivory with cotton clouds, but streaked red when he blinks and hears the bonfire crackling and mingling with the shouting.

Shadows over him. Human-like. One, two, three. All known, but he can't tell them apart. Four. *Who's missing?* Five: blue eyes amidst a face grimy with blood and murk. *Murchaud's alive...* Scowling and snarling and prying open Cellach's jaw, shoving something hard into his mouth and kneeling on his right arm. He frowns and wrestles but there is pressure on his legs, on his hips, on his left shoulder—crushing him against something hard, dooming like the gait of the woman at his left. *Sláine.* Standing grim, hauling her sword and dropping past the border of his vision.

Somewhere, the bonfire crackles.

Someone screams and it rumbles on his chest, on his skull, on his throat behind his wooden muzzle and once more because she's standing, bloodied and hauling her sword, plunging again. Murchaud slams Cellach's head into the hardness underneath—and he can't turn to look, can't escape, just thrash and howl while something presses against his left arm and brands him from the inside out, blasting, burning, blinding and suffocating with a sweet-sour decay, acrid and coating his throat while he kicks and breathes that greasy heat, legs thrashing and jerking alongside the war-drum of his heartbeat. He writhes again, tossing savagely, thrashing and kicking but easing amidst the petrichor of the grass, the breeze hurrying—pungent and sharp-scented like pines.

Wrong, so wrong. So suddenly painless. *Why?*

Words. Ill-shaped but spoken, above the pain and past it.

Words. Booming on his mind, but decanting onto him. Scattering into the forest and wiping the shouting, the voices, the noises, the faces, the shapes, the stench of his stump burned to save his life.

Words, echoing past the rustle of leaves between bushes and branches and the harsh slashing of his jagged breath.

Wood on his mouth, or perhaps just the pressure of his jaw, the chafing of his teeth. Saliva, thick and choking and pooling at the base of his tongue, dry and musky but bloodless and halved by the cool breeze. *No... no, no, no.* Clean and without blood, without the stench of heated iron against his skin.

"No, no..." The words tumbled from his mouth. Trembled. "No! No!!"

Cellach rolled onto his left shoulder, the arm still outstretched in a desperate reach—towards the pine with a shadow-man crouching under its canopy, above that shroud of fog-smoke and its amethyst shimmer. Halved, the left arm. Cut past the elbow and dressed in leathers, no longer bleeding, no longer burning although his eyes closed aflame with shame, with guilt, with the frustration knotting his throat, with the failure trailing through his cheeks. No longer blazing, but still bearing the delirium of pain and the shame of being less.

Half a man.

Him.

Cellach

Marching. Unsteady over that shroud of amethyst fog-smoke coiling around his tired feet. *Mind-rot, a curse, or a sign.* A chuckle twisted sour in his mouth—like his saliva, burning and full of bile. *A sign of what? Decadence?*

He shook his head. Refused to look around and search for the shadow because finding it or not would be evidence of his state—damning evidence. *As if that waking nightmare hadn't been enough.* At least he'd been alone in the forest, his shame kept private while he thrashed in the ground. *More reasons to hurry towards Gleann Mór.* Yet his arm still itched on the wrist that wasn't there.

Itching.

No. Just mind-rot, that itch.

Burning and itching. Gnawing. Ruthless.

Ignore it. Like the shadow. Walk to—

Itching, itching, itching and creeping until Cellach contorted his arm, grinding the stump against his chest—right, left and back though the angle was wrong and the relief a cruel tease.

Just scáthcuma[1]*: the grief lingering like the shadow of what was.* Itching, itching, even that word. Meaningless and hollow because what he felt was too real, too certain, too itchy and aching with that crooked weight and the—

It is there; the shadow. Look at it. But he didn't, couldn't. Just pressed his maimed arm across his torso and trudged on—gaze etched ahead, refusing to move. *Look at it!*

Pines to his left. Spindly branches, darkness underneath and the remnants of fog below—silver and moonlit, but shimmering amethyst over the grass-blades. Thicker than before, like strands coiling away from him. *But the Fidnemed... it never fogs. And the shimmer, that—* His throat tightened; thickened his saliva and burnt when he swallowed. *—the amethyst shimmer, before it never... I never saw...* His gaze edged left while he trudged ahead, looked left, stepped on, left, onward, half-left, left— *There!*

The shadow-swordsman. Threading the undergrowth and matching his crippled pace despite the screen of trunks between them. *Twelve, fifteen feet away,* but close, too close and looming although it never so much as glanced in Cellach's direction. *What if it's not my mind rotting away?* A knot twisted on his chest, halved his breath. *Spirits, if this is you... your curse, your blessing...*

Nothing.

Nothing but the dull thudding of his footsteps, lighter on his left side. Nothing but the breeze chilling his sweat-dotted neck and pulling his jaw, easing it left, guiding his gaze.

Nothing but that shadow-swordsman now watching him.

Eyeless, though everything else was there. Leather boots, scarred poleyns, leather vest, uneven vambraces. *That armour...* A shield on the left arm, a sword and a knife on his belt. *Is that my—?*

---

1. Author's Note: For scáthcuma I mixed two Old Irish words: scáth (meaning 'shadow' or 'shade') and cuma or cumnha (meaning 'sadness' or 'sorrow'). Cellach's translation as "the grief that lingers like the shadow of what was" is not meant to be literal, but the concept his society represented with this word.

A pinecone burst under Cellach's foot.

He groaned, veering around a fogless, smokeless pine. His thighs throbbed and begged for mercy, but stopping was not an option—not until that shadow was gone, not unless he risked capture, not without the threat of being hauled back to Dunlow. *Hundreds dead on my command... and they still want me as Chief.*

Not without meeting their gazes again.

It hadn't been horror what he'd seen on his warriors after awakening; that had only contorted his own reflection. Hadn't been pity either. *Worship.* Devotion because he'd survived everyone's nightmare. *But only half of me did, mind-rotted even.*

Cellach looked up, between the coils of amethyst strands, past the thinning canopies and into the buttermilk sky. Artanem's claw twinkled faintly, marking the path back towards Gleann Mór. *The Spirits guide me.* Even his warriors believed it; perhaps all of Dunlow's forces. *Touched by the Spirits, they say.* He'd heard it whispered when he awoke, feverish and embittered by the joy in their faces—the relief on Murchaud's blue eyes, the respect in Sláine's greys. *They're fools. All of them.* Fool enough to consider it a privilege to come wash his burnt stump with yarrow and honey, or later wrap it in beer-boiled linens. *Half a year since those healing rituals, and yet I'd rather drink piss than beer.*

Drink. Piss, water, anything.

For too long he'd only swallowed saliva.

A grunt tore from him, instinctive like the hand falling onto the waterskin at his belt. *Softened cur.* Yet he still licked his teeth, looked down and down and down to the amethyst coils swirling around his feet.

Inexplicable. Irremovable.

Oozing left towards the shadow-made boots an inch from his own. *What does it want? What should I do?* His gaze refused the looming silhouette, etched in the twig-littered ground—though his knees quivered, his legs, his hand. Quivered because the breeze—*Is it breathing?*—found every drop of his sweat and chilled it. *What is that shadow?*

His mouth parted, hanging ajar but speechless.

A curse, a sign... which one? How to find out?

Closed, grinding his teeth.

What should I do?

Nothing. Just stillness. *Keep walking*—so he staggered forward, thighs burning, calves taut, face wrung in a scowl. His stomach growled, hungry. *Three sips, three jerky strips. That's all.*

He didn't stop. It was not an option.

Run, stay, pray, strike, wait... what? Spirits, what!? Something locked Cellach's legs, forcing him to stop. Etched his gaze on the red-barked pine ahead—contorted as if reaching for the crooked moon high above. *I've waited too long. Must act. But how?* He chewed his parched lips, tasting the scabs and ripping one with his teeth. *It has changed, that shadow-swordsman. Changed quicker since crossing the Teifi.*

It'd been a month since it'd appeared back in Dunlow, first a scar in his vision and then a shapeless mound he thought a remnant of a nightmare... until it'd grown legs over the days, arms, detailed hands, braids. A hawkish nose with a familiar scrunch. It never reached for him, instead watching and following, oozing that amethyst smoke now condensed into strands.

I should face it. Ask: 'What do you want?' A scowl furrowed his brows, lingered in his indecision, in the tremor of his jaw, of his fingers. *No. Cannot risk giving offence if it's a Spirit.* In the twitch of his cheek. *Look at it. Decide later.* He snapped at the forest beyond.

Pines, just like before. Spindly branches, darkness underneath each, and shafts of night but no fog, no amethyst coils, no shadow-swordsman. *Where is it?* Pines, branches, shadows, no fog, just grass. *Is it a test, then?*

Peace suffocated him.

A sudden, abject peace.

The shadow-swordsman. It had returned.

Marching a few rows of trees to Cellach's left, but closer. Closer like the griadergh, dawning eastborn over the needleful canopies. Closer, and matching his crooked cadence.

Run, stay, pray, strike... steer left?

Cellach risked a glance.

Walk towards it or wait for it? Shouldn't risk giving offence. He swallowed. *What if my silence is an offence?*

Another glance.

It could be an evil Spirit. The Storytellers talk about them.

One more—but the shadow-swordsman did not turn, did not react, did not change its pace.

Cellach looked ahead. Breathed. Risked a last glance.

The Fidnemed was empty. Full of shafts of dawn searing the remains of night. *Nothing there; just—* He shut his eyes, shook his head and kept trudging, kept walking. *Must reach Gleann Mór, leave Sláine and the others behind.* His tacky tongue darted through his lips, his gaze returning to—

Pines, pines everywhere. Red-barked, twisted, needleful and gloomy, some full of rot and fungi. Spindly branches, pinecones, twigs in the ground. Shafts of blood pouring from between the canopies, then shafts of night pooling into shadows, into shapes.

Fog, as well. Moist like its petrichor. Not amethyst, just vibrant violet. Violent.

Just pines, branches, shadows, no fog. Just grass.

Prayers tumbled from his lips—broken noises, no meaning, no sounds, no shapes, just ill-born half-things drifting into whispers, into silence, into nothing at all. Injured by the pressure wringing his chest, crushing his breath. *What to do?*

The shadow-swordsman didn't react—standing four paces

ahead and staring at him with the same copper eyes Cellach saw in his every reflection. Unblinking, but convulsing with molten fury and the maelstrom churning inside him.

Grief. Remorse.

I let the Aelorians burn the rune-marked trees of Gleann Mór. Blasphemy. A sin like no other. *Excused it on needing to regroup, to wait for reinforcements, and then charge in a second attack.*

Guilt. Contempt.

Couldn't even keep my promise. He'd returned later with more warriors, with more weapons—but he'd retreated again with half his units and half of himself. *Craven. Worthless. Weak.*

Shame, shame, shame.

Disgust.

Burning in those eyes, spilling like molten metal and drowning him until his heart staggered—wrenched in half yet somehow full, full and swelling with emptiness, with fury and everything swarming the shadow-swordsman's eyes. Cellach's eyes.

"Please…" Torn from him, a thread of his voice, of his meaning. "Please…"

Silence. Absolute.

Itching like his stump. Itching, itching and maddening, itching until the shadow-swordsman twisted its mouth—a half-grimace, half-snarl drowned with everything melting in the furnace of its eyes: contempt, disgust, loathing. Eternal, that stare. Abyssal even as it stepped aside, stretching its whole, right arm to point a path—framed by red-barked pines, the ground littered with twigs and pinecones but marked with footprints and steering northeast.

"Walk."

A command, in Cellach's voice or perhaps stated by him because he mumbled and mumbled and only mangled noises tumbled from his mouth—not-quite words, not-quite prayers either but meaningless, hollow because he'd left half of him in Gleann Mór and all he had know was contempt, disgust, loathing.

"Walk."

Run, stay, pray, strike… No. None. Just walk. Walk for now.

One step, sideways. Swallowing hard, bile that burnt his throat. *Spirit?* Then another. Mouth parted, ajar and trembling and speechless. *Or evil Spirit?* Yet he couldn't know, just edge around the shadow-swordsman. Rounding it, aiming for the signalled path. *Does it matter?* Slow, so slow and careful and aiming for that road, watching those eyes of molten copper. *No, it matters not.* Trudging backwards, locked in that stare. *It's a Judge, regardless. My Judge.*

Cellach

Wading. Careful. *Keep walking. It hasn't ordered otherwise.* Barely lifting his feet off the ground. Deliberate not to traipse and touch any of the sacred trees surrounding him. Leafless, all—just trunks engraved with runes and stained with coal. Mingling with fuller ones and spreading as far as he could see. *A blessed path. The Judge's path.* Full of rune-marked trees only found in the Fidnemed and towards Gleann Mór like guidance from the Spirits. *From the Spirit's Judge. Where is it?*

The urge consumed him. To glance around, to search for it. *No, it's there, somewhere.* It had to, because the fog-smoke poured from him, just an amethyst shimmer flowing with his every trudge, weaving leftwards. *The Judge is there. Don't look.* Unworthy, that was why—or perhaps he couldn't stand the loathing in those lookalike copper eyes. There was a reason he avoided his own reflection when—

Footsteps. To his left.

Resounding for the first time since the shadow had appeared.

The Spirit-Judge's? Steady. Marching beside him, loud and firm and muffling Cellach's own with a rhythm he could no longer achieve—weakened by his exhausted heart, by aching legs and the swollen feet jailed in murk-stained boots. Slowed by everything else weighing down upon him.

Guilt. Regret.

Remorse.

I ignored it. For a month. Lurching from the darkness of his mind. *Should've approached it sooner.* Eating him. Snapping his gaze from one tree to another—here, there, back, right, back again, left. *Don't!* Ahead. He looked ahead amidst the fitful hammering of his heart, his unsteady march leaving footprints on his wake.

It waited, the Spirit-Judge. Until I reached this blessed path. Full of sacred, rune-marked trees leading northeast towards Gleann Mór. *It's all by design, by the Spirits' design.*

The breeze. Cool or warm and clinging to his throat with the coppery tang of— *My arm. When Bran burnt—* His palm slammed against his mouth, and he swallowed saliva branded with bile, with tar and burnt iron. *Not real, just mind-rot.* Slipping past his fingers, the greasy sweet-rot of—

Cellach groaned. Held his breath while he trudged—but the stench endured. Acrid, oily, heavy.

"Weak. Assaulted by memories…" That loathing was familiar in its hues of inbred disgust. It came from his left, rippling through the amethyst shimmer: "Haunted by the shadows born from your shame."

The Spirit-Judge! Cellach's heart slammed thrice. *Answer, answer, answer.* But he opened his mouth and nothing came, all words dead on his throat. The truth couldn't be refused.

He was weak.

Weak, because game sizzling on a bonfire turned his stomach.

Weak, because he'd retreated—*Twice, twice!*—and let the Aelorians burn the sacred trees of Gleann Mór. *Blasphemy!*

Weak, because when his punishment had arrived, he'd succumbed to the echoes of yore, to the waking nightmares and the breeze always clawing with the stink of—

Scáthcuma.

But his legs do not answer to him, his feet do not carry him onwards because if he moves his left arm will swing. Half-there, half-gone. *A test. It must be,* though he's uncertain because he can't trust what he feels, what he smells or hears or sees. The weight, the stretched skin, the cold slipping into his shattered, open bones. It aches, burning, each finger curling half-dead then half-alive and spasming—

His face contorts. Eyes shutting, mouth pursing, jaw clenching taut. *A test from the Spirit-Judge.* Throbbing on his cheeks, on his neck, on the hands, both fisted. *No. Just scáth—*

"Every waking moment without half your arm… yet you still confuse the truth." The Spirit-Judge, breathing on his nape, on his shoulder. Chilling his sweat. "It's gone. Gone."

His arm.

Gone.

A test, Cellach knows, feels it too. *Penance for my shame.* But the hand is there, clenching so tight his nails scrape the calloused palm, shaking with anger, with power, with the weight of the shield fastened to his forearm. Tight, the non-straps, and pulsing with the broken hammering of his heart— there, there, not-there, there again. *Not real. Just gone, gone, gone—*

"You lost it." Strangling him with words, snatching his elbow with an iron-grip. "Yet you can't stop thinking it's there."

"Scáthcuma." Cellach's excuse, thin and feeble and weak and worthless but the only thing he has. "You test me."

Laughter. Chuckling, twisting, choking, crying, sobbing.

He hears it, hears it fully. All the meaning of it.

Breaking, chortling, chuckling. Sob-laughter.

Self-blinded because his eyes are shuddering half-open and he grinds them shut, keeps them tight until the stars throb opalescent in the darkness of his mind.

"Look down." The Spirit-Judge, distraught. Clutching his elbow but stepping around because the footfalls are there, hammering the words. One, two, three, turn, stop. "Look down. It's not there. You lost it."

No, no, no. Numb from the elbow down, numb from that

choking grip. *Yes, yes, yes.* Numb, numb, numb even though needles prickle his forearm and wrist and every finger—

"No. No!" A growl tears from him, sour and ferric like the bile and the blood he spits to his right with his eyes still closed. "I lost… more than that. I lost—"

"Half of you." Regret, remorse. Guilt in that voice so akin to his own. "The good half."

"Echoes, shameful because—" Choked. Hacking and hacking until something streamed from the corner of Cellach's mouth: acid, iron, wetness. Wetting his cheek and pooling on the ground; mingling with his words: "They s-survived, the echoes. N-not me."

Chuckling, drowning. *The Spirit-Judge's.* Suffocating.

Pouring onto him through the amethyst smoke.

"I'm still…" Harsh, acid, dry. Pressure in his chest, iron on his mouth—he'd rather have that than the truth. "I'm still there… in Gleann Mór."

"Still there. Under that shield, with the hand in your face." The Spirit-Judge, grim and certain and truthful.

Cellach sucked in a breath, choked with the bile he dragged back into his mouth. "It was the same in Dunlow." He was lost. Like his voice and the will to stand and walk again. "I just want — b-back. Into the battle. Why?"

Noises. Leather rustling, a scabbard hitting the ground.

Cellach blinked. Dragged his gaze to the Spirit-Judge: crouching low before him like an echo of what he'd been… or not, perhaps not. Because one forearm rested atop his bent knee and the other dangled between them—half-torn but half-there, dead, not-there, heavy, light, burning, bleeding.

Perhaps it was just a reflection of who he was, smeared in that amethyst shimmer—thin, thinner than before, almost gone.

Blood, bile, saliva.

Leaking. Wetting his cheek.

"Just a broken remnant." The Spirit-Judge pointed at him with a dead-finger, a non-finger. "Survived, but cannot live.

Why?" Amethyst, poured from that dangling hand, from both of them. "Why, why, why do you want to return?" Silence. Overwhelming. "Only that answer will set you free."

Night again. Blindfolded, starless. Choking him with that stench—twisting his gut with bile but making it growl with hunger, with cravings, with disgust and agony and the thick, greasy stink of game blistering over open flames. *Tests, more tests. Just—*

"Weak old wardog. Snared into the same pit of mind-rot." The Spirit-Judge, pouring loathing over him. "Stand up! Smell the real world!"

Twigs and rocks drove into his shins, the poleyn's straps tight behind his knees and pulsing with his heartbeat—broken, hurried, looser, tighter. Wrenched in half and refusing him. *Don't breathe. It's just—*

Grease, fat, blood boiling. Flames and food and laughter and that look of awe, of reverence, of—

No. Not now.

Dark, musk, sweet, reeling past him and blurring at the edges because someone kneels before him and smiles. Grey eyes, bright with awe, with respect, with a request for forgiveness never asked. *Sláine?* She's there, kneeling before him, offering something, saying words—blurred, all of it, blurred because all that matters is the thing in his mouth.

Grease. Smeared across his lips, staining his moustache.

Rotten, smoky, wet and greasy like death and oil and a trail of salt and iron turning his tongue into ash. It burns his throat and he gags, hacking and instead gobbling it down, down, down into the bile creeping through his throat, swamping his mouth. He gags. Again. Lurches and retches because—

"Dragged back through the filth of what happened..." The Spirit-Judge, quiet but deadly and full of the disgust churning in his gut. "You owe me an answer. Wake up!"

Blood. In the grass. Besides his hand and mixed with bile, with saliva, with the emptiness in his stomach. Blurred by the amethyst mist wrapping his left arm and slithering on and on and on to the Spirit-Judge.

Close but far, standing upright and scowling at him with those copper eyes. Full of molten fury, of loathing.

"Smell it." It snarled, jutting its head to the northeast—where the canopies thinned and the stench came through. "What if it's real? What if it leads you to the answer?"

Cellach frowned. "Why?" Coughed. "Why… do I want to return?"

Laughter rumbled somewhere north. Real, perhaps.

Cellach

Walk. Right foot, even. Left, half-dragged. Again. Again and pursing his mouth, swallowing a groan because the breeze was cool and chilling first, then warm and reeking of roasted game. *Ignore it. Walk.* Right, left, onwards. *Follow the path, go to—*

"You never think of the aftermath…" The Spirit-Judge's voice came from behind—calm, restrained. Landing closer like its footfalls.

Cellach kept his eyes forward, unworthy of anything else.

"Why?" It insisted, unhurried as if the response existed already.

Not the same question, Cellach knew—then hesitated, licking his lips with a tacky tongue. *Or perhaps it is.* He kept moving, silent and assailed by a hundred answers, all curling and twisting while he trudged past one tree, sharp-scented and full of leaves. *Can't remember, that's why. It's all a blur.* Round another, emaciated and rune-marked. *Liar. I remember waking… but the months blurred after.* Under thinning canopies, between two others and a third, while his legs shook and his heart twisted into a knot. *Liar, again. I remember agony, crying, retching, itching, awe, disgust, drinking, dying, waking.* Gravel crunched under his feet. He slipped beneath a branch, waded through the sweet-sour stench in the breeze—greasy, heady, charred. *Just lay awake for days. Thoughtless.*

"Your answer?" Immutable, the Spirit-Judge. Expectant.

"Because—" Cellach coughed, clamping a hand across his mouth and breathing before whispering: "Because I'm a coward."

The stench still filtered through, perhaps with noises and the crackling of flames. Perhaps with the voices he'd heard.

"That's not the answer." The words marched from behind him, level and inevitable. They spread like blades of ice cutting through his sweaty neck and claiming his mind. "Try again."

Still, Cellach didn't turn, just walked. Right, left, steady. *Not the answer, no.* Steadier the more he thought, rubbing the stump against his swollen chest—the amethyst mist poured from it, clouding a path towards his left. *To the Spirit-Judge. It waits for the answer.* He kept his gaze on the pines. *Answer.* Glanced into the thinning canopies. *Try again. Answer.* Matching the hammering of his heart with his steps and that command he refused to carry.

Answer, answer, answer.

"I know what happened..." He whispered at last, gesturing to his left arm without daring to see it. It itched, maddening, itching, burning, itching— He coughed. "How it happened. I don't need—"

"Wrong answer." It was the Spirit-Judge's voice, but Cellach's also—rising from behind him, slithering through the amethyst strands. "You keep avoiding the truth." It prickled at his neck, chilling and indomitable and full of loathing. "Not remembering the aftermath, the pilgrimage to Gleann Mór... there is one reason behind them both. Which?"

The instinct to turn clawed at him—and Cellach halted, shut his eyes and pumped his fist. *Not the same.* True, true, true, or so he wanted it to be, needed it to be. *It is not the same.* Lies, lies, lies because he'd escaped Dunlow and his armies driven by a single need.

"I need to return there, to—" Broken words, broken meaning. *Not the answer.* His mouth moved, settling lower than before. *I know the answer,* and it teased in the darkness of his mind, amidst the mind-rot he couldn't clean. "Because..."

Gaping, lips trembling. Not quite a grimace, not quite a silent howl of sorrow.

Answer!

Silence.

Answer!

The breeze saved him, condemned him. Slipping between his moustache and bringing that stench again. Greasy, heady, fatty, roasting in the flames—

Gagging, choking, retching, retching and wrenching the truth.

"Because I know who I was before. After that..." He choked —with the stench, with the words, with everything swelling within him and the bile burning his mouth. It tore the truth from him. "After waking... there was nothing. Nothing left, nothing... of *me*. Just the need to find what I left in Gleann Mór."

Something gripped his shoulder.

Curiosity bested his reverence, and he looked down—to the ink-woven hand half-dissolved into a mere outline of shadows. To the forefinger struggling to raise, to tighten, to point ahead. *Where—?*

Nowhere, gaze still locked in that hand. *Ahead?* Impossible to glance further back, as if Death waited there. *Why?* His pulse pounded in the silence, booming on his chest, on his neck, on his temples when his eyes cut from that pitch-black shape to the amethyst mist and to the path ahead.

Pines, rune-marked and needleful, all mingling, all red-barked. Twisted, gloomy, braced by bushes and shrubs and opening into a clearing—bathed in moonlight, so silver and plentiful that nothing interrupted it.

Cellach swallowed, and in a reflex not yet forgotten, he gripped the hilt of his sword and trudged forth. Quiet, as quiet as he could, with his breath held and steering towards the shadows spilling under a pine. His right knee popped when he dropped into a fighter's crouch, legs throbbing in tandem with the hammering of his heart. It pounded erratic, swelled and warped while his gaze sifted through the blurred, silver expanse before him.

Pristine grass without footprints. Bushes at the rim, a hare or two slipping under a shrub. Pines, rune-marked or full of leaves, but all twisting away from the darkness at the clearing's centre.

Immutable, that darkness.

Raising towards the nightsky but untouched by the moonlight.

A drulock. Not found by coincidence, but by design. *The Spirit-Judge's.* Standing somewhere behind his back, where the amethyst mist—a mere shimmer of stardust—ended. He almost looked, but didn't. Stopped short of glancing over his shoulder when laughter burst from the clearing, easing his soreness, his doubts, and the weight he'd dragged since departing Dunlow.

Everything eased, just because he knew that laughter. *Disgusting,* like the words that followed, rumbled in a language he'd heard before but never understood.

Aelorians. Somewhere there, sitting around a bonfire and corrupting the most sacred place of all: a drulock. *A door for the Spirits to come to this world.* One tale among many shared by the Storytellers, yet one he did not doubt. One he could not allow to be marred, though it'd require stepping into the—

"Your next answer is there." A bare whisper, hissed near his ear but gone like the hand. "The question: what did you leave behind?"

His heartbeat assaulted him. Pounding in the silence, booming on his chest, on his neck, on his temples when his eyes cut from his cover to the drulock and pines surrounding the clearing. *The next question.* Exhaustion rippled through his knees when he rounded the tree, careful to stay under the safety of the canopies and away from the clearing's pristine grass. *The next answer.* From there he crept forward, testing the ground with each step, moving quietly. *Find it. Answer the Spirit-Judge.*

Amok

SOUL TRANSMUTER ALCHEMIST. THE UNTAMED ONE

The moonlight bathed the clearing, drenching the rune-marked trees with a shimmer of starlight. It smoothed the hues of blood sprayed across the ground and blended into the amethyst mist surrounding one unusual man.

A survivor. An exception.

He was holding a sword and ignoring the corpses at his feet to stare at the Shadow standing beside him—the most detailed incarnate so far, albeit smeared into rivulets of shade.

A most fascinating moment, and one Amok had sought for a thousand years—so they observed, crouched atop the drulock and glamoured to invisibility amidst a shroud of glyphs. Jade, cyan, ruby.

All bursting with possibility.

All awaiting the moment that could prove or disprove one hypothesis.

"Answer me," the Shadow hissed, raising its mangled left arm towards the northeast. "What did you leave behind in Gleann Mór?"

The subject dallied like all humans did, thinking themselves above the passage of time while being nothing more than ephemeral sources of alive elements. Thoughts, emotions, questions, attitudes—they swarmed him with grief and relief, with regret and respite, with fear and desire and the echoes of yore still strangling him, yet slowly losing their hold on him. A maelstrom in itself, spreading like rivulets of a hundred violet hues and merging with the remnants—the mist—of amethyst Strands.

"What did I leave behind?" The subject repeated, scowling at the corpse sprawled at his feet, then at the one he'd thrown onto the fire to smother it—only to smile, sweet-sour. "Who I was. I lost… me… *him* in Gleann Mór."

Silence, during an unforgettable night, under the silver shimmer of a crooked moon, in a world which had started anew not long ago.

Silence, while the Strands shimmered like stardust, that mist thinning and trimming until it evaporated into nothingness. His body collapsed, dropping to his knees then onto the right shoulder—yet as he plunged, the Shadow evanesced as well, its blackness gone without a trace.

A ruinous conclusion.

A moment of reckoning.

The most salient outcome after a millennium of persistent inquiry.

The Untamed One grinned, and the gesture sliced their featureless non-face, revealing the abyss within. Rippling with displeasure at the failure and delight for the results, with rage at a flaw yet unresolved and rapture for the implications. Brimming, wholly, with ecstasy because a successful incarnate was finally—*finally*—within grasp.

A thousand glyphs burst from the galaxy within them, swarming the alchemist and begging for their attention to further the research. Cyan symbols for questions considered and demanding revision, jade ones for answers finally encountered, and ruby ones—invaluable all—tempting them with shards of the Uncharted.

Amok reigned them all, letting them follow while they hovered down from atop the drulock to alight near their latest subject—Cellach: the only human to experience an incarnate soul-skill and almost survive it. He seemed peaceful in his death, with his copper eyes half-closed and his mouth curled in a nascent smile. There were no traces of alive elements in him—

for they all vanished with death—but the glyphs had recorded the relief that'd washed him before he perished. The one behind that smile.

The very same relief that had dissolved the incarnated Shadow, causing his demise.

His demise. His death.

A most regrettable flaw, calamitous because it'd marred an otherwise successful outcome, haunting because it ought to be solved at all costs.

Grievous, but perhaps comprehensible—so Amok flicked their wrist, reorganising the glyphs. They swirled around them, aligning by priority and preference until the jade ones—the answers—repositioned closer.

The first one, brighter than all the others, represented a change the alchemist had introduced at the experiment's outset —one deemed risky at the time yet overdue in hindsight. Instead of sundering the subject's self all at once, Amok had slowed the incarnation to weave the amethyst Strands day after day. This had built Cellach's bodily tolerance, fostering his curiosity until he had, at last, accepted the Shadow.

A pivotal moment, reflected in the second jade glyph that moved forth—an answer, albeit dimmed into a filthy hue of green full of Amok's contempt.

It represented the subject's reason for such acceptance and a limitation of humankind. The ubiquitous need to disregard the unknown by abusing an indisputable label: divine intervention. Humans depended on it because its mere use neglected the possibility of understanding the Uncharted, thus allowing them to punish those who dared chart it. They preferred to live in ignorance—deeming it respect for the sacred—because it was safer and easier than grasping their own insignificance. Throughout all ages, throughout all worlds, humans had preferred to believe rather than to comprehend in fear of the only possession worth having: knowledge.

Amok crushed the glyph in their fist, jade sparks leaking between their fingers. That abhorrent tendency had allowed Cellach to explain and accept the Shadow, while misunderstanding a fundamental part of himself. Regardless, it had enabled the incarnate to continue—

"There! Chief!" A man's shout, brimming with shock and threatened hope. "I found him! Sláine, here!"

Half-turning—and still glamoured to invisibility—the alchemist traced the clearing's curve with their gaze, stopping on the hulking, blond warrior under a rune-marked pine. His hair was braided back, his leathers rustling while he paced at the moonlit edge, pointing to the three corpses. Just like the woman beside him—black-haired and silver-eyed—he remained oblivious to the alchemist's presence, even as they soared to stand atop the drulock amidst their shroud of ink and glyphs.

"Chief!" She shouted, pacing, restless. "Chief!"

Intrigued, Amok extended a hand, summoning a handful of glyphs and gesturing them forward. They darted through the air, swarming the woman as she ran towards Cellach amidst a thunderstorm of alive elements. Doubt, faith, distress, hope, dread, desperation—a dozen hues of it, volleying with the despair induced by grief, the anguish of guilt, and the torment of never offering an apology.

"Chief, hold on!" Her trot faltered, her agony slowing her down until she knelt near the body. "We're here, we—" Denial strangled her. "No." Grief. "No, please no." Regret, misery. "How? Why!?"

Her emotions melted into the expectant glyphs, blending with the blond's—now trotting across the clearing. He slowed, aghast as he took a knee beside her. Desperation swarmed him as well, albeit with more remorse and another flavour of guilt.

The Untamed One watched them, rolling two fingers to lock that handful of glyphs into the humans—observing and documenting the events which, albeit Natural, were likely trivial to their research.

Strengthening their invisibility glamour, they returned to the glyphs surrounding them—rearranged into neat columns, their intensity reflecting their priority and relevance. Among them, an entwined trio hurried forward, landing on Amok's hand to reveal three flavours of the same matter. One flared cyan with a hypothesis partly solved, another jade with a limited answer, and the last one… lingered untinted.

Untinted. Unasked, unknown, unfathomably absurd like only one thing could be. One *unsolvable* thing, impossible in its existence.

Their intrigue leaned towards that untinted complication, but the alchemist focused on the cyan glyph instead. It represented their initial theory, and the one that had led them to research the incarnate—for a soul-skill that allowed a human to interact with their own alive elements, embodied in a Shadow, could potentially ameliorate the mental impact of those elements, and reveal unknown depths to the alchemists.

A provocative inquiry, so complex that even Cellach's success had failed to fully resolve it. Regardless, the jade glyph—almost melded to the cyan—was a partial answer and the source of Amok's delight, of their rapture and their ecstasy. It represented inimitable success: for this human, a Chief of a nameless group of warriors in a world too new to be of relevance, had—at last—interacted with the Shadow and partially soothed the distress it represented.

A singular breakthrough, long awaited.

A leap of immeasurable magnitude, verging on proving Amok's theory… if only for its most regrettable flaw—a blemish in an otherwise ideal result, an unexpected defect that could not have been prevented because it was not yet understood, even after a thousand years, even after hundreds of subjects and a methodical, Naturalist process.

Not *a* flaw, thus, but *the* flaw.

Offensive. Vexing. Fascinating like nothing else.

The subject's demise, his—

"Why did you die, Cellach!? Why!?" The woman howled, desperate in her ignorance and with a grievance Amok nearly mistook as their own. "You killed them, so why!? Why did you die…"

—death.

Inopportune. Incorrect.

Irrational, because everything suggested it should not have occurred. Unexplainable because the knowledge needed to do so existed only in the abyss of the Uncharted. Unsolvable, as per the untinted glyph, because it was a paradox Amok could not solve. Yet.

A paradox.

The Untamed One trapped the untinted glyph in their hand, grinning at the iridescent shimmer within it, at the myriad of contradictions creating that paradox.

Before Cellach, hundreds of subjects had died because they'd failed to accept the incarnated Shadow—but he'd died after *accepting it.* The others had been failures of the process, while he had been a failure of success itself. He had interacted with the Shadow—the embodiment of the self-deprecation caused by the loss of his arm—and had effectively assuaged it by discovering the answer it needed only to die... a fundamental outcome contradicting what happened Naturally: were a human to placate their thoughts or emotions—alive elements both—they always survived.

Survived.

Why?

The glyph sparked in the alchemist's hand, iridescent.

The same action—ameliorating one's own alive elements—ensured survival if achieved Naturally, but had caused death through the incarnate.

Why?

Amok hooked their forefinger beneath their first thumb, snapping the iridescent glyph—it chimed, melodious and unperturbed. Refusing to yield any answers and instead haunting the Untamed One with more questions.

What if the flaw had not been Cellach's, but Amok's? What could have the alchemist misconstrued in the theory of the incarnate? What shard of the Uncharted did they need to unveil to find the answers?

The glyph twisted again, pulsing and brimming and splitting into six new glyphs—three cyan for the questions just posited, three jade for the evidence that fed the paradox instead of resolving it.

Yet their grin returned, savage like the abyss within—eager for answers, for an avenue towards the truth of that paradox, for the knowledge needed to chart one more shard of the Uncharted.

There was a flaw to correct, but even then Cellach's success had been undeniable. Through him, Amok had confirmed the benefit of the lessons learnt through his predecessors, while providing the fundamental pillars of replication: tolerance for pain, curiosity about the unknown, acceptance of the unexplainable, and the primal need to understand oneself.

What remained was not a flaw—just the need for more research, for new experiments that would unravel the paradox.

There was no other possibility, no other pathway, no other plausible conclusion for Amok's nature did not allow it. After all, their desire for the Uncharted was untamed.

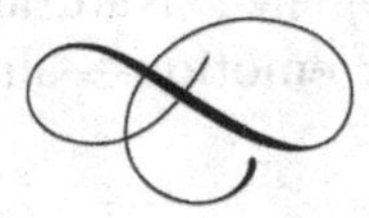

Corvalen Caelands

1473 Bonn Era (BE)

Amok

SOUL TRANSMUTER ALCHEMIST. THE UNTAMED ONE

Power exceeding the limits of comprehension.

Inexhaustible as to twist the confines of the universe and bring the most absolute existence into a newborn realm. It twisted the known and leashed the world to its will, piercing the nowhere into the where to anchor on the drulock with threads of the purest cobalt. It commanded reality, folding the universe to connect unfathomable distances and pour the power only one had Charted.

At the edge where present became past, Amok built their Integrity Shield to protect their *self*, scribbling a thousand cerulean glyphs—each shimmering with the reverence and respect that forced them to kneel before the only alchemist who had surpassed them all: The Rector, the commander of The Orders.

They descended from the cobalt threads, their obsidian cloak fluttering on their wake as they alighted onto the drulock's roof. The feathers cascading from their golden pauldrons shuffled with the motion, while those crowning them fluttered and tightened over their abyssal hood. One blade hovered beside each arm, but it was only the scimitar that edged towards Amok.

'*Untamed One. I see your research has progressed...*' Their voice was plural and omnipresent, lingering like a test of will.

Amok pressed both hands into the roof beneath them and bowed in silence, for it was a rule never to speak in front of The Rector unless explicitly asked to. Yet amidst that prevailing calm, they risked a glance at the humans below—carrying Cellach's remains towards the clearing's edge while oblivious to the alchemists' presence and the threads folding the universe.

'I have a question for you.' As The Rector mind-whispered directly to Amok's mind, the scimitar spun on its axis—and the cobalt threads pulsed in tandem. *'Have you found your next subject?'*

There was nothing at the seam of becoming—just the Untamed One glancing again at the departing humans, then raising their cerulean eyes to stare at the blade before them. Something was charted on it, knowledge that even in plain sight exceeded their grasp, knowledge even more foreign than the pattern of existence engraved on The Rector's breastplate.

Yet past that seam, desire teased Amok to mind-whisper one question: *'Could one assume... The Rector has a suggestion?'*

The leader of all alchemists chuckled, and that sound rippled through the cobalt threads anchored in the drulock—threatening to curb the universe with plans only their endless existence could exploit. *'I have indeed... and she's part of a complex mission I must entrust you.'*

A hundred glyphs burst from Amok's cloak, sinking into the galaxy within them before surging with another question: *'Is it here in Nuu?'*

'In Lambda, which you haven't visited yet.' The Rector flicked a hand, charting a topography on the scimitar's blade. *'That world is steering into self-destruction, Amok, shattering the balance we have so carefully imposed on it. You'll meet your subject while resolving such a discrepancy. She is... interesting.'*

Before the magnitude of the statement struck Amok, the scimitar shifted again, replacing the topography with the profile of a woman—with caramel hair streaked blonde, and azure eyes as deep as an ocean. She seemed to be reading, the weight of understanding tensing her brows.

The Untamed One released a glyph from their cloak, capturing her semblance. *'May one ask...'* Daring. Daring because in all their existence they'd never imagined The Rector could use such a word. *'...why is she interesting?'*

'Your experiments have not covered someone like her,' The Rector stated, unchallengeable like the power that kept the universe folded. *'She has the potential to transfigure as an alchemist, so you will recruit and train her, Amok... and in the process solve that paradox that so perturbs you. A successful incarnate is finally within reach.'*

The paradox.

The paradox?

Discovered mere moments ago, yet already known to The Rector—the commander who, since time immemorial, had manipulated existence beyond Amok's comprehension. As they doubted, the image on the scimitar blurred when the woman looked aside, instead reflecting the cobalt threads.

'Return to The Towers.' The Rector commanded, soaring airborne while their voice dispersed into four mind-whispers. *'Another alchemist awaits you there; they'll collaborate with you in correcting Lambda's course... while completing a mission of their own.'*

When all words vanished, only the threads remained, pulsing with anticipation. The Untamed One observed its length, from the anchor in the drulock to the shimmer piercing the sky. It folded the universe, making accessible the inaccessible: The Towers, the bastion of The Orders of Alchemists.

It was a privilege to undertake a mission for the leader of all alchemists, a mystery to unravel what they'd deemed interesting, an unparalleled opportunity to resolve a perplexing paradox—so Amok stood at the rim between the known and the unknown, between what had been and would be.

One impasse, and they crossed the edge of certainty.

Author's Notes

Thank you so much for reading *The Echoes of Yore*, and for your interest in my Author's Notes.

This was quite an interesting book to write, and it ties up directly into the first entry of the series: *The Omens of War*. Therefore, I wanted to use these Notes to touch upon some of the ideas I explored in this novella—a brief behind-the-scenes, if you will. It won't be in depth, but I hope you'll find it interesting.

PS: There is a freebie at the end.

On verbal tenses and their meaning.

I must confess something: to me, grammar and sentence structure add meaning to the text—something that cannot be conveyed through words alone. Thus, I set myself to experiment in this story.

But let me start from the beginning.

I originally modelled Renan, Sian, and Cellach with different degrees of dissociative post-traumatic stress disorder (PTSD) in mind. In particular, dissociative PTSD flashbacks are intense, involuntary re-experiences that involve depersonalisation, derealisation, and the loss of dual awareness—often causing the individual to lose the ability to simultaneously recognise they are living in the present while the past feels as though it is happening again. That sensation of unreality is what I wanted to capture here... and perhaps something else, given the speculative side-effects of Amok's research.

With this context, logic would argue that I should've chosen *past* tense for the dissociative flashbacks and *present* for the story. I did the opposite and had a reason for doing so.

On the one hand, third-person past-tense narrations are common, and even when writing a limited narrator they feel somehow controlled and detached. On the other hand, third-person present-tense narratives are unusual and destabilising to the reader because they bleed events into the realm of 'happening now' and—quite literally—breach the narrative agreement of past-tense.

That feeling of intrusion, of wrongness bleeding into the now to *become* the now was exactly what I wanted to convey, so I... just took the plunge and used present tense for the flashbacks, while relying on continuous tense (e.g., -ing) or base verbs as 'stepping stones' to smooth the transitions (if needed) from one to the other and back. In other cases, I relied on repeating the same verb in both tenses (Sian's opening chapter does this).

ABOUT AMOK'S EXPERIMENT...

As you read this book, you may realised something: Renan, Sian, and Cellach were *not* the protagonists. Their experiences may have been at the forefront, and their misadventures may have moved the plot forward ... but this story wasn't about them as much as it was about Amok's experiment and the paradox they unveiled.

So what *is* the incarnate?

If you're new to *Records of The Orders*, I'll explain without spoilers: Amok belongs to an Order of alchemists whose abilities and interests are derived from psychology and philosophy (particularly Sartre, Kierkegaard, Stoicism, among others). Since these alchemists explore and manipulate 'alive elements'—thoughts, emotions, attitudes, identity—Amok has been trying to develop a new way of studying them: the soul-skill named *incarnate*.

They hinted what it did at the end of Chapter 2: "[the incarnate] required sundering the self to stream it into a vessel, the Shadow, and ensure its autonomy [...]" and at its purpose at the end of Chapter 3: "[...] a soul-skill that allowed a human to interact with their own alive elements, embodied in a Shadow, could potentially ameliorate the mental impact of those elements."

You may ask: What was I thinking when I came up with this idea?

Let me tell you.

We can argue that our sense of 'self,' or identity, comprises different *facets*: interests, reactions, attitudes, and ways of thinking that interweave to create the whole person we are. Some of these facets can also take the form of maladaptive coping mechanisms—patterns we develop in response to traumatic events. These mechanisms may include (but are not limited to) reacting with self-criticism (as Renan does), trying to explain traumatic flashbacks in a rigid way to hold on to a sense of reality (as Sian does), or blaming oneself for not behaving exactly as before the trauma (as Cellach does).

Therefore, since my alchemists are—first and foremost—researchers of questionable ethics, I asked myself one question: what if one of them tried to 'extract' these maladaptive coping mechanisms to 'embody' them in a semi-autonomous entity (the Shadow) and have them talk to the person to see how they reacted?

That is how the *incarnate* soul-skill was ideated.

It may or may not have been loosely—*very* loosely—based on chair-work from Schema Therapy. It is not, nor does it try to be , a faithful or accurate representation of it. After all, I'm just a writer who likes to speculate.

WHERE DO WE GO NOW?

The Echoes of Yore is one of the many entry points for *Records of The Orders*. As a whole, the series is a genre-blender: psychological horror, alchemists obsessed with knowledge, unusual takes on morality, philosophical concepts as part of a secondary setting, brutality that's neither explicit nor voyeuristic, and what you have not tasted in this novella: high-level political intrigue and military settings.

So let me ask you a question: **Where do *you* want to go now?**

To follow the mission The Rector had for Amok, I suggest you dive straight into the first book of the series, *The Omens of War*. It happens immediately after *Echoes...* and Amok is a point-of-view. However, one word of advice: *The Omens of War* is complex. It'll drop you into a politically and philosophically elaborated setting affected by an Uncharted not yet revealed. I wrote it as a puzzle-box, and hope you'll enjoy it as such.

That said, to discover how alchemists are 'made' (what they call it 'transfiguration'), you can read *The Genesis of Change*. It follows two alchemists while they experiment on humans... and it's fully written from their perspective to explore how they see the universe. That novella also visits The Towers of The Orders —a place where past, present, and future exist simultaneously. It's far more philosophical, but it'll give you a good primer on alchemy before you dive into *The Omens of War*.

Better yet, the ebook of *The Genesis of Change* is free for my newsletter subscribers. I write monthly (or every other month)... with something pretty unconventional: thematic secrets of this series, deep-dives into the meaning/imagery, reading lists of non-fiction I found interesting, and even symbology and clues.

If either of those piqued your interest, just scan the corresponding QR code and find your next read:

That said, I honestly hope *The Echoes of Yore* interested you. Thank you so much for reading.

Livia~

About The Author

Livia J. Elliot writes dark and thematic fantasy, with an emphasis on character development and meaningful themes—especially struggle, control, identity, self-perception, and bias. She's currently releasing two series: *Records of the Orders* (weird, philosophical fantasy) and *Tales of the Bookshelves* (psychological fairy tales for adults).

She is also the lead writer of *Unearthed Stories*, an app publishing interactive fantasy and sci-fi for adult readers. On the side, Livia also hosts the podcast Books Undone, featuring literary analyses of speculative fiction.

If you enjoyed *The Echoes of Yore* and want to learn more about the universe, receive exclusive sneak peeks, and a free prequel novella, then **sign up for Livia's newsletter** using the QR code below, or filling the form at https://liviajelliot.com/newsletter

www.ingramcontent.com/pod-product-compliance
Lightning Source LLC
Chambersburg PA
CBHW011929050726
47591CB00009B/2409